Y0-CXK-245

Cold Comfort

by

John Becker, S.J.

authorHOUSE™

1663 Liberty Drive, Suite 200
Bloomington, Indiana 47403
(800) 839-8640
www.AuthorHouse.com

This book is a work of fiction. People, places, events, and situations are the product of the author's imagination. Any resemblance to actual persons, living or dead, or historical events, is purely coincidental.

First published by AuthorHouse 03/28/05

ISBN: 1-4208-3643-9 (sc)

*Printed in the United States of America
Bloomington, Indiana*

This book is printed on acid-free paper.

Cover image by Winston Hewitt.

Acknowledgements

Cold Comfort would never have seen the light of day had it not been for the patient help of many friends. I am grateful to each of them.

John Becker, S.J.

ONE

Father Luke Wolfe put the key in the lock and with a sigh opened the classroom door. He swung it up against the wall so that it would stay open and slowly walked—almost shuffled—to his desk by the windows.

He put his battered briefcase on the desk. And the bag with his breakfast from the Snackeree—the students' campus Dairy Queen rival.

It was obviously a pleasant day—mid-seventies–with only a single delicate contrail to heighten the virgin blue of the sky. The mockingbird who had taken up residence outside the classroom window in the jacaranda tree was doing his happy-go-lucky thing—completely upstaging the awkward scolding of the surprisingly ugly grackles and the timid chirps of a cactus wren unhappily trying to steal some attention from the prima donna. But Father Wolfe was almost oblivious to them.

It had been a long night—short on sleep. When he said Mass just before coming over to the school, he could scarcely concentrate on what he was saying—much less even try to conjure up the presence of God. Deep down he knew he would make it through the day—he always did. But his present muggy head had him wondering if he would.

"Hiya, Father." It was Tony Santos, his huge eighteen-year-old frame filling most of the doorway. He was smiling a welcome with his whole shaved head.

"How're things?"

"I was surprised you weren't there when I opened the door. I thought that that had become your job. To be there to welcome me and all the tykes to ROOM 102, KINO PREP, PHOENIX, ARIZONA, in the morning." Father Wolfe had capitalized it with the extra emphasis of an old-time circus carney and eyed Tony in gentle irony.

Kino College Preparatory was the name George Wheatley had insisted on when he founded it in 1928 just before the Depression to end all depressions. He adored his wife, Helen, and when she had died the year before, he had insisted on a fitting memorial to her and had invited the Jesuit Fathers in to do their school thing. George had been both lucky and wise. He had brought grapes to the Valley and just to the west of Phoenix. When Prohibition had arrived, he had turned to grape juice and after 1933 returned to wine. The wine—Arizona's Finest—had flourished and soon rivaled the California vintages both in bouquet and sales. And his clever radio ads had the kids singing their tunes. Now this large building—the architects had been savvy enough to tie the Old Mission style to a touch of Arabic and their own imaginations—was a tourist's delight. It was a familiar sight to see an amateur photographer with another state's license plate snapping pictures of the Jesus statue in the front courtyard and the chapel behind it.

And since Eusebio Francisco Kino had been the extraordinary Jesuit in the late seventeenth century who under his leadership with his fellow Jesuits had evangelized and civilized northern Mexico and southern Arizona all the way up to Casa Grande—the

Great House—which the Indians had built centuries before and he had named—it seemed only natural to dedicate this Arizona Jesuit school to him.

The original two-story complex–initially intended to be a college and then a university—was a large H. The college hopes had died with the bruising of the Great Depression. But George Wheatley's dream had survived in the college-preparatory high school that was now Kino Prep. The prayerful chapel—with the bright stained-glass windows that shifted and changed the Arizona sun much like St. Chapelle in Paris—was the binding bar. Above all this, standing happily in the sun was the bell-less bell tower.

Father Wolfe smiled. How long ago was that? Five years, when five-foot-tall Michael Reddy had so very seriously approached him after class and asked the obvious question. "Did the Swedes give the architect the no-bell prize for our tower, Father?" With his eyes alone he smiled ingenuous innocence. And he was gone.

And Father Wolfe's classroom looked out on the white statue of the Sacred Heart of Jesus standing over a small pool just to the west of that chapel. His first-floor classroom was on the south side of the northwest leg of that huge letter. The Jesuit residence was the other side of the H.

"I hadda escort Rita to Mother Teresa's." Tony hunched his left shoulder a bit, as though he were moving someone out of the way. "Too many guys on the way to and from our sister school who might want to make time with my girl." And his fear was undoubtedly justified. Rita didn't have the classic beauty that made it to women's magazine covers—her Barbra Streisand nose attested to that. But she was very pretty. And pert with her Barbie Doll face. But there was something more to her. A woman's knowledge of who she was. And how she stood before Almighty God. Her mature goodness seemed to shine through every gesture and word.

Rita Poulos had been "his" girl ever since the end of football season. "We were over at Mass at St. Ignatius next door—as we promised you—when?—two, three weeks ago? Right now she hadda see her Latin teacher, Mrs. Bokes, before she heads over to Mother Teresa. She's there—upstairs in her classroom." He lifted his head slightly to indicate just where that was.

Father Wolfe smiled a more enthusiastic smile—he was coming to as he did every day when he met the students. It had been a delicious treat to have two adolescents—on their own—receiving the sacraments to keep their love right with God. And what was especially fun-filled was that he the priest had not even mentioned this Communion—the Jesus-gift of Himself—to them as a possibility.

Mother Teresa College Prep, Father Luke knew very well, had come into being just five years previously. He had been there when Kevin Klein, by the grace of God Bishop of Phoenix, had dedicated the first building. The Bishop had wanted, he said, in a Catholic way to bring education—in at least one diocesan school—into the current mode of educational thinking—which was, ironically, the old way of looking at it: that adolescent boys and girls learned better when they had their classes separately. Less of the wrong kind of competition. And greater ease at concentration. And saintly Mother Teresa being the role model for all girls, he named it for her—even before she would likely be canonized into Saint Mother Teresa. And since Kino was an all-boys school, it was only logical that its feminine parallel should be somewhere close: the students from both schools could enjoy the discrete ambiance of the classroom—although they shared two or three classes in each school. And the social mixing of extracurriculars. And just hanging around together after school.

"Or out of jealousy I often consider the proposition that they might take her away from me." Tony grinned. Like the happy Heinz tomato—even if Tony was hatless. And not so rubicund. He was big for his eighteen years, and stocky. It was a football lineman's build.

"And then there's Larry Curtland. Ever since she talked to him in jail, whenever he sees her now he gets stars in those already green eyes of his. I don't mind his thinking she's gorgeous. And an angel. She is. But I don't like those stars—green stars. I'm afraid he might feel the urge to try to take her away from me. Jealousy, it's called, Father."

TWO

What was it Frank Vogel had said? His best friend when he was attending St. Luke's High School in San Francisco—was it sixty years ago now? They were double-dating that night, taking in the big bands—on records of course—dance at St. Catherine's down in the Mission. He could no longer remember the words that had started the mischief. Had there been any? But it was Frank's grin, the happy grin that had loosed the green-eyed monster in his heart. Frank had been dancing more with Janey Peers—the girl Luke was wild about and had been dating for six months—than he had with his own date.

And every now and then the other dancers would stop and open a stage in the middle of the dance floor and clap Frank and Janey encouragement in their elegant gyrations, apparently floating free of any earthly gravity, Frank smiling like a little kid whose parents had finally bought him the toy train—with the real smoke and the real whistle and the switches and opening-and-closing crossing gates—gift he really wanted for Christmas, Janey, skirt swirling and face flushed, looking as if the gates of heaven had opened to her. Fred Astaire and his Ginger Rogers revisited. Which left Luke to dance with Frank's date, Sally Enfield, a nice girl, a pretty girl, but not his Janey. Frank, the tall basketball star, the movie star–handsome young male with the bright blue eyes and tanned skin and wavy blond hair. The girls put on a swoon act at the mere mention of his name. And he was going to take his Janey away from him. Father Luke bit his lip at the memory and straightened the few strands of white hair on his almost barren pate.

And so Luke had planned to trip Frank as all four of them were walking down the broad cement stairs in the poor light after the dance. And thus a broken leg would end Frank's basketball limelight career—at least for that year. There was not much thought about it. He had to do something. That was clear. And the only way was right now: cripple him. Clearly. Definitively.

Stupidly, too, of course, because he knew that every woman loves to mother the sick, the crippled.

And only at the last moment when Luke was prepared to sham a stumble and stick his foot out to catch Frank's, Janey suddenly stepped a little more quickly than the rest of them. Right between them.

Had she known?

Sixty years later, Father Wolfe found his face burning with shame. Did he show it?

The next day when they met at Luke's locker, Frank had grinned, the left side of his mouth considerably higher than the other. And laughed. "Thought I was gonna steal your girl, didn't you?" And suddenly Luke had known that it was all just a tease. Jealousy, yes, he knew all about it. And often when he went to confession, he would again tell Jesus in the priest his long-since malicious desire to really hurt another human being. Schadenfreude gone amok.

"Yes." What else was there to say? He understood very well Tony's fear: it was so very easy to return to the past for only the few moments the memories lasted.

And then Father Wolfe's mind went back to Tony's opener "How're things?"

"Well, last night was"—he laughed a bit—"a little difficult."

THREE

The night before, Father Luke Wolfe had awakened with a start. And now the whole mélange of what had resulted refused to leave his mind alone. He had turned over to look at the bedside clock. 1:57. Had the air conditioning imploded? It seemed particularly warm. Was that why he couldn't sleep? No, it was too early in the year for it to be doing its cooling thing.

Maybe he needed some food in his stomach. He lay there with his eyes closed and considered the matter–he hadn't really eaten much supper. He was tired, but he wasn't sleepy.

Finally, he had swung his feet over the side of the bed, pushed them into his thongs and gasped as the arthritis in his seventy-eight-year-old body insisted that it would not be an easy thing to get to the closet door and a robe.

Down the stairs to the kitchen of the Jesuit residence, the other leg of the Kino H–opposite his classroom. Slowly. Slowly until those legs caught up with his intention. Into the walk-in fridge. Nothing much here—big jar of Vlasic kosher pickles. He had always been puzzled by that word. If kosher had to do with pork, what was the title doing with pickles? Had he missed some obvious link? Couple of quarts of milk. Two pitchers of iced tea. A bag of Idaho potatoes. A huge glass bowl full of salad for lunch.

He pulled a Miller's Lite out of its carton on the floor. Well, that was at least something. But there was no sign of ham or cheese or bologna to frame with two pieces of rye bread.

Maybe he could find some hamburger meat in the walk-in freezer next door. Microwave it up into something that would get him some ZZZZs.

Light switch on. With a heave he had pulled the freezer door open, pushed his way through the heavy plastic curtain striated into what must have been fifteen seven-feet-long translucent vertical leaves.

Hamburger patties and bratwurst were usually just inside the door to the right, next to the Eggo frozen waffles. Not there.

He lifted packs of frozen fish fillets. And solid bags of chopped onions, baby shrimp.

No hamburger. No brats. Nor anything of their kith or kin for that sandwich. Nothing.

He looked up to the left. And gasped. Lying against the back wall in front of the frozen bread and cartons of orange juice concentrate was a mannequin like the ones just inside the dress shop windows of any mall—right arm outstretched as though tossing flower petals to the adoring crowd, head back, left arm akimbo on the jutting skinny hip. Then Father Luke smiled with relief. Who could have played this dumb joke? Or was there some good reason to freeze a mannequin? He looked again, and suddenly realized that he was looking at the body of a woman, wearing some kind of red shift. He blinked and gasped again: it was a woman soaked in blood and apparently frozen solid. His old legs seemed about to sag beneath him. His breath became stertorous.

He shook himself out of his shock and put his finger on her jugular. To see if there was still any pulse. Pointless. Of course she was dead.

Then he noticed the small gold crucifix on a chain around her neck. A Catholic? So he conditionally gave her the Sacrament of Reconciliation—if the soul was still there—so that God in His mercy would forgive her whatever sins there were.

Arthritis now distraction-dulled, he had rushed over to the kitchen telephone—although he later wondered why there was any hurry—and dialed 911. As he was talking to the operator, it suddenly occurred to him that he would have to go out in front of the house to tell the police where to come—there were so many entrances to the school. He found himself confused with the local geography he knew so well.

"Dead. But you had better send the paramedics anyway. Kino Prep. 5800 block of Kennedy Drive. North. East side." And then he remembered that he should update Father Brown—Louis Brown, the Jesuit Rector, the superior in the house. Louis would—as he always did with every challenging dilemma—take quiet control of this macabre situation. In the middle of the night: it was 2:14 by the kitchen clock. Up to the second floor of the Jesuit house. Past Father Pierre Atkins' door with the "Gettin' old ain't for sissies" sign. He knocked on Father Brown's door—loud enough, he hoped, for the Rector, but not loud enough to awaken old Father Pierre next door—he was in his early nineties, and he needed all the sleep he could get to maintain his enthusiastic outlook on just about everything.

Father Brown took in Father Luke's wheezing—he had climbed the stairs too quickly—"In the kitchen walk-in freezer. Frozen. A woman. Lots and lots of blood. A corpse. I called the police. Have to go out in front and let them in—when they come."

As Luke expected, Father Brown was as imperturbable as ever. Louis Brown was short and on the chubby side with a round little-boy face and almost no hair left on his head. But no one who knew him thought of him as a child. Behind the little-boy looks, there was a brilliant mind—his senior theology classes sat fascinated as he showed them the relationship between everything from Adam to Pope John Paul II—and candid concern for everyone he met. He threw on a robe and followed Luke down to the freezer.

When the police came, there were a lot of questions. Well, it was really only the young lieutenant—Lieutenant Higgins, Lieutenant William Higgins, that you could see was all business tonight with none of that "old alumnus" cheer, even though he had been in Father Wolfe's class ten, twelve years ago. He was slim—with a still-flat stomach—and tall and very serious and wanted to know all sorts of things now. What was Father Wolfe doing in the freezer? Did he usually do that? What time was it? Who else could have gotten into the building and then the freezer? Father Wolfe felt himself grow hesitant under the grilling. The tables were turned. He had been the one to ask Billy questions in class.

"Billy"—it had been early September, and Father Wolfe was passing back paragraphs the sophomores had been asked to write the night before—"don't you have a spell check on your computer? Didn't your teacher last year teach you even the simplest punctuation rules?"

"Well"—Billy was discomfited—"yes, Mr. Frankle did go over and over the stuff in class. But, like, nothing seemed to grab hold."

"But you could at least have called up the help of the spell check."

"I couldn't find it, Father. I'm not one of these computer geniuses."

What could he say to that kind of riposte? "Billy, re-write the paragraph and write out the misspelled words correctly and the simple punctuation rules you have shredded—as they are stated in our Kino English Grammar"—three years before, the English teachers had spent most of the summer designing a very simple grammar that weeded out all the abstruse and debated points of the English language and contained only what they really wanted the students to know when they graduated. "I hope that will help your memory problem."

And now Billy was asking the questions, and Father Wolfe wondered if he was doing any better than sophomore Billy Higgins had. Was Billy smiling a little behind his serious face and questions, now that the roles had been reversed?

Yes, who else could have gotten into the building? And so, very much with the help of the banister, he had had to half-pull himself up the stairs again. This time to Father Friedl's room—he was the Father Minister, the one who, with all of his other household duties, locked up the house at night—to bring him down for Lieutenant Higgins' questions.

At 4:30 he had dragged himself up the stairs again, this time to his own room. He felt totally deflated from exhaustion.

FOUR

When the alarm exploded at six, Father Wolfe dragged himself out of bed, dressed, shaved, said Mass in the community chapel.

Now, his briefcase under his arm, down the steps, down the hall towards the street.

He was met at the front door by what looked like a dance-hall repertoire of flashing lights—red and blue. Three or four police cars supporting them. And puddling out from them was a Fire Department boxy paramedic van, and one of those business-like mortician vans they use to cart off the remains and pretty it up before they do the final business from the back of a Cadillac hearse. And a plain sedan. Probably the doctor's.

They took up so much room that the students' cars could only trickle past to get to their parking places next to the canal.

Down the front steps, through the cloister next to the chapel. Suddenly he was hungry.

Not surprising since my midnight fridge foray went amok and there had been no time for breakfast.

He headed through the chapel vestibule and over to the Snackeree at the edge of the gym.

"Do you have anything like a Danish? And coffee? And OJ?"

"Right here, Father. Does that look all right? Cream and—"

"Black. To go."

"I'll put caps on them, Father, and everything in a bag." The student worker behind the counter—it was Joey Schmartz—smiled. "That way you won't spill it."

FIVE

"Father." Father Wolfe was back to the now. It was Norm Balinski at the door. "Kin I use one of your computers?" They lined the classroom walls, all thirty-five of them, for in-class essays.

And they were a timely semi-modernization of the classroom. A classroom that was festooned with memories. Ship models: one year—long ago—they had been reading one of C. S. Forester's Hornblower books. And Jacob—what was his last name?—and his brother Harold had found and bought kits and built three Horatio-era men-of-war. Airplane models hung from the ceiling. A poster on the wall urged students to do good things: like: Put a quarter in an empty parking meter. There was the Esso tiny-tiger balloon that someone had brought back from his summer Europe trip. Besides the usual crucifix in each classroom, there was the brutally graphic chiaroscuro litho of a painting retreatants had found on the wall behind the altar of their retreat chapel in the full-of-God-in-nature retreat house to the north of Phoenix in a canyon of Sedona's red-rock loveliness. The Christ was in twisting agony and naked—and at the same time fitting and decent. The blacks and whites and grays underlining the pain and abandonment somehow better underscored what the God-death was all about. And there was the talking frog by the doorway. Jimmy Jagozinski had brought it in one day after he had bought it at a Walgreens drug store. Whatever its initial message, Jimmy had taped it to say: "And where do you think you are going, young man?" And that in a deep Louie Armstrong gravelly voice. Its activity was turned on by any motion within six inches in front of it. And it was so placed that a casual turning on or off of the light switch would bring it to make its demand.

And so the computers neatly complemented all of this. And somehow modernized it—to keep up with the times. They were the huge donation from Anthony Antler. Matt, his oldest son, had been in Father Wolfe's class and told his father about the older computers Father Wolfe had been using. He had graduated just two years ago. Anthony Antler ran a huge engineering firm—Cyber Inc.—and was constantly updating the high-tech stuff and gave Father Wolfe his "old" computers. That, and a lot of time with the help of Xavier Carroll, an adolescent computer genius, had given him the start on this work station for class writing.

Norm seemed forever in a dash to finish a writing assignment at the last minute for one teacher or another. Always at the last minute. "Economics. For Hairy Rabbitt. Oops! Mr. Harold J. Rabbitt. But you must admit he is hirsute."

Where did Norm pick up that esoteric word?

"*Why The Market Has Turned Sluggish.*" In a reverent voice he capitalized the first letter of each of the title's words—even the article. And italicized it.

"Of course, Norm. I didn't know the market had turned sluggish. But you are welcome to use a computer. You don't have to ask."

"Mother always told me to be polite. Where do you turn this here one on?" Father Wolfe felt too tired to correct the solecism.

"Just to the left. The button on the power strip." He had told him just a few days ago, and he had forgotten so easily. *What's with this cyber-generation?*

Had it really become an intellectual cryo-generation—frozen solid in the face of any kind of logic? Or was he just getting old and skeptical of anything young? Was cynical *a better word?*

"You know us intelleckchoowals, Father: the sordid details are beneath us." His laugh sounded like a sousaphone coughing.

"What was the difficulty?" Tony had not been distracted. He was back to Father Wolfe's comment before Norm had arrived.

And Father Luke told him all that had happened the night before.

Students with their backpacks began to enter the classroom in ones and twos. Tall and short. With collared shirts and baggy shorts and gym shoes—the last often untied and flopping on the ground as they walked.

"Morning, Father."

"Hi, Father." Some dragging. Some laughing just for the sake of laughing, bubbling over in the joy of their own vital juices.

SIX

"Hey, Father, what's with all the police cars and stuff in front of your house? Did they finally catch up with you guys and your connection with the Mafia?" Andy Sarlin—wildly disheveled hair all over his head, his face with a continual toothy smile sneaking out—could never be serious.

Father Wolfe laughed. "No." Should I tell them what was going on? Too complicated. How could he briefly explain a woman's corpse in the Jesuit Residence? "Probably looking for you, Jer—with a few questions about the Snickers you stole from Brad yesterday."

"Aw, Father, I just borrowed it." Andy laughed a syllable or two.

SEVEN

Then, two voices in unison.

"Father." It was partly question and partly—somehow—fear.

At the doorway stood identical brothers, sophomores in Father Wolfe's second-period class.

"Yes, Terry. Yes, Barry."

"Hey, you guys must be twins." Tony loved to tease the freshmen and sophomores. And somehow he sounded as though he hadn't picked up the whole story even though he had met them the summer before.

The look-a-likes regarded one another as though they were strangers. And the look made it clear: they did not want to talk to Tony. But they were too caught up in the game that was like a part of their soul in each of their lives. "No. We're not twins."

"Well, you certainly look a lot alike." Which was true enough, of course, save that Terry looked as though he never combed his hair at all, and Barry's mop seemed to have been combed but only hesitantly and with a rake. And there was Terry's cleft earlobe. A slight difference, hardly to be noticed. But they were both no more than five feet tall and wore identical round, fair, Charlie Brown faces—like the roseate faces on the cherubs the old Italian painters used to love to surround the Holy Family and other Saints with. And today cap-à-pie their clothing was exactly the same: collared yellow IZOD shirts, brown cargo shorts—the kind with many apparently useless pockets all over them—almost invisible socks and blue-and-white Reeboks—laced.

"Well, you're brothers." The twins' bodies twitched as one in an effort to get back to the point of their being here in the first place.

"Yes." It didn't seem to matter who answered.

"Tellmetellme."

"We're triplets." Terry paused just long enough to look Tony in the face to see if he had registered the joke. "Our sister Mary goes to Mother Teresa." Father Wolfe—who had heard the conundrum resolved so many times—smiled. Tony guffawed—his whole large body enjoying his mind's appreciation. Of a joke he had heard but had forgotten its punch line.

EIGHT

The first time the two boys had come into Father Wolfe's life was the summer before. After his grades had been turned in, even though Mr. Arthritis—Luke's ever-present companion in pain—protested violently, he had put up shelves two feet wide—just room enough for the monitors and computers—and a neat twenty-six inches off the ground—on all four walls around the classroom. On them he set up as many computers as possible. And even though Matt Antler had been the sophomore with the brightest and happiest and most destined-for-greatness look on his face, but never seemed capable of coming up with a correct answer, his father's gift of the "old" computers had proved exceptionally valuable. Pentium Ones. Not the fastest on the market but just the thing for student writing during class.

Big Xavier Carroll with his big laugh—he seemed able to laugh at everything, even when bad things like flunking a calculus exam came his way—and lean frame and carrot-red mane that stumbled all over his head—had stopped by Father Wolfe's classroom after the last classes of the year. He had not been in Father Wolfe's class as a sophomore or as a senior, but one of his buddies who was told him of Father Wolfe's difficulties with his new gift.

"Can I help you with your computers, Father? I have a little experience with programming them." And that comment quickly proved to be a massive understatement.

"I certainly could. Whatever you know about computers, it is far more than I do. I need them all networked—tied together somehow. And I need them so programmed that students will not only be able to create on the computers in class, but look into—but not be able to change—one another's work. An excellent tool for class essay writing and correcting and teaching at the same time."

And Xavier quietly showed how much he really did know about computers. The two of them worked for the rest of the day.

The next day Xavier phoned to say that his grandmother had died and the whole Carroll family was going to go back to Detroit for the funeral—leaving that day. But Xavier had been accepted at Notre Dame, and he was supposed to start caring for the campus grass and other herbaceous pretties on his work scholarship there the day after the funeral. Which left Father Luke trying to reach Xavier long distance for this advice and that. Computer programming was just not the old priest's forte.

NINE

"What's with this sudden departure of the Dean's secretary? Mary Kucera."

Three days after Xavier's departure, the Jesuit supper table had been the usual potpourri of talk and eat and listen and learn.

It was Father Joe Garcia, aggressive freshman algebra teacher and enthusiastic freshman football team coach. As he worked on his third helping of corned beef, he raised his eyes and looked at each of the other priests at his table. "What I mean is, why did she just get up and leave at the end of the last day of school? No goodbyes to anybody. Just suddenly she wasn't there." He shoveled in a forkful of cabbage as though he and the cabbage were enjoying a long friendship. "Didn't Phil"—Phil Van Steen was the Napoleon-like—both in physique, if a little more rotund, and demeanor: it was enough for him just to say something to student or teacher to ensure that it would be done immediately as he wanted and when he wanted—Dean of Men—"like the way she did things?"

"We still don't know." Principal Gerry Sloan raised the glass of wine to his lips for a very careful sip. "We still don't know why she left."

"Well, I always found her to be"—Pat Gallese (he said Guh-LEES) loved sophomore algebra classes so much and so obviously that the parents of his students often joked that they too would like to be students in one of his classes—"one of those classic no-nonsense secretaries."

"Phil will have his hands full without her help. For the rest of the year. And during summer school." Al Friedl wiped his mouth. "Unless they can find someone as competent as she was."

The other table of Jesuits next to the huge mural of the great Southwestern Jesuit missionary, Eusebio Francisco Kino—astride his horse and wearing his black cassock and flat Roman priest hat and herding a huge passel of longhorn cattle—erupted in laughter. Father Pierre—he was an ebullient 90-year-old—shouted the punch line again. "And his father wanted him to be a trash management driver because even when the economy was bad his business would always be picking up." More guffaws. Somebody banged the table.

It wasn't so much the joke he told: Father Pierre has a Bob Hope gift for the adroit pause, the wry smile, the whole theater of mimicry and huge enjoyment of the irony involved.

Al Friedl was sitting on Father Luke's right. "How's that computer network in your classroom coming?"

"Whenever you needed some information, she would quickly pull it up on her computer monitor." That was Pat again.

Father Luke tried to come up with a quick answer. He wanted to tell Al that his star computer quarterback had already left for college, but Luke did not want to bother his fellow Jesuit because every summer Al spent most of the vacation in his physics lab designing, revamping and repairing his fascinating demonstrations of the physical laws of God's universe.

This, besides taking care of the physical needs of the Jesuit community. But his mouth had just taken on a fork-full of salad.

"And whenever you make a mistake in sending her the day's absentees, she quietly and calmly and with a big smile made the correction." That was Father Chris Weigel—he was getting along in years, but still taught an enthusiastic moral theology class to five classes of juniors, and he was always having trouble with this new-fangled computerized attendance-taking.

"Where's Walt tonight?" That was Father Brown, always concerned about "the family" being at home and together for supper as many nights as possible.

When Father Luke had finally managed to masticate the lettuce, his answer to Al was quick. And despondent. "Awful. I have lost the one computer hack who knew what he was doing. And ever since I have been foodling"—Father Wolfe obviously liked the dictionary-shy word, so much did he use it with its onomatopoetic fun—"around with what he told me and achieving nothing."

"He was killed in a train wreck this afternoon." Andy Beauchamp—he said Bo-SHAMP, and when he said it, it somehow implied that he was twirling the end of the minuscule French mustache which he did not have—somberly started work on his apple pie. "You knew how afraid he was of flying. So he took the train. And it derailed just this side of Santa Fe. Ironic."

"And the computers are doing everything but what Xavier said they should." Luke hadn't been listening. And now became aware of the sudden silence of the rest of the table.

"I didn't see anything on the evening news about a train wreck." Al frowned.

"Hi, guys." Father Walt Kahn had gathered a bowl of split-pea soup, a salad plate and corned beef and cabbage plate from the buffet offerings. He put all these—he relished showing how adroit he still was at his high school job of waiting on table at Denny's—in front of the empty chair, crossed himself, blessed the food and sat down. "How're things?"

"What gives? Andy just said you were killed in a train wreck this afternoon. I don't understand." Al had stopped eating and looked straight at Andy.

"You don't really fall for Andy's macabre jokes, do you?" Walt turned a wan smile across the table at Andy Beauchamp. "After all, even St. Thomas Aquinas had room for a *mendacium jocosum*—a joking lie. I translate for the benefit of you—um—younger men who have not had Latin." With his head down he looked up over his eyebrows at the rest.

"My trip today was from central Phoenix to here—my usual route from office to home. And I just got in from the law office—huge load of unfinished business this afternoon." He laughed. And made a move on the split-pea soup.

For a moment or two the table was silent.

The neighboring table erupted again. "And the golden telephone to God in Ireland wasn't $10,000 a minute—as it was in all the other churches of the world. There on the auld green sod it was a local call." Father Pierre Atkins was at it again.

Dan O'Malley produced a groan so loud it washed over to Luke's table. "The Irish ought to be ashamed of themselves." His affected brogue sounded straight from Killarney.

"Why don't I see what I can do for you, Luke." It was a statement.

"Well, I heard that Mary's husband teaches over at Mother Teresa, and with all of those young and pretty women teachers over there she wanted to protect him from a serious case of roving eye." Pat was not to be distracted.

"What's with the corpse, Luke—the one that was making our fridge look like a cemetery mausoleum?" Walt Kahn was dusting his salad with olive oil and vinegar and sugar—Joe Garcia winced as he watched—and salt and pepper.

"Nothing much new, Joe."

TEN

But the next morning of that summer—it was Saturday—promptly at 8:10—as though they were still in school—Father Al with his Vandyke beard, infectious enthusiasm and quick eyes was suddenly standing beside Father Luke in his classroom, ready to rescue him. Father Wolfe thanked St. Peter Canisius for bringing him this wonder—as he did when anything worked in the new media of his classroom. St. Peter had been the first Jesuit to get a book published—one that became a super-best seller in his time—books, of course, being then the latest media presentation of his time, almost five hundred years ago.

And as Al directed and Father Wolfe worked, everything began to drop into place. They had worked for two hours, maybe three, when Father Al suddenly sat down, his hand on his chest. "Luke, I think maybe I'm having a heart attack." His face was gray-white. His voice went weak. "You'd better call the paramedics."

And when they came, they had confirmed Father Al's own diagnosis, and then rushed him off to St. Mary's Hospital.

Luke had first phoned Father Brown the Rector about what had happened, then rushed over to the house, and the two of them headed down to the hospital, only to find that Al was already on the operating table. It turned out be a quadruple by-pass that was needed, and the job had been done just in time.

They were still sitting in the waiting room when Doctor Joe Ganss—the surgeon who had done the cutting—came in, still in his greens and funny hat and mask hanging down over his chest. Father Wolfe was reminded of little Joe Ganss who had a terrible time with the difference between *lie* and *lay*—was it twenty years ago?

"Father is fine. He has a good, healthy body. And he should soon be out of the recovery room. There's no point in staying now. He will be sleeping until tomorrow, probably."

"Did his work in my classroom bring this about?" Luke knew it couldn't have, but he worried anyway.

"What were you doing, Father?"

"Programming computers."

Doctor Ganss smiled. "No, I don't think so. I'm surprised from the look of his heart that this hadn't happened much earlier." He smiled. He laughed his soft laugh that somehow seemed to match perfectly his short, stubby stature, a laugh that said that everything would be all right. And he was gone.

"Why don't you go home, Luke? I know Doctor Ganss said there was no point in staying. But I'm still going to stay here for a while. There's nothing more you can do while he's in the recovery room. And I will let you know when to come down and pick me up to take me home." Quiet, competent Father Brown always seemed completely unflappable, no matter the situation.

Which left Father Wolfe in a bind again. St. Peter seemed too busy about other things besides networking the computers in an English classroom.

He tried to follow Father Al's instructions—in fact, he was sure he had followed them to the letter—and everything worked. Except for the final most important tying them to one another and the printer.

ELEVEN

Two days later, while he was in his classroom trying to resolve this frustration in programming these wonderful and mind-boggling Anthony Adler gifts, these two roly-poly boys who now stood at the door had casually walked in and introduced themselves. To all appearances they were both in fourth grade.

"We're the Mohr brothers. And we..."

"...have you for English next year." So they weren't fourth-graders after all.

"We're going to summer school..."

"...but if you need some help with your computers..."

"...we'd be glad to assist..."

"...in any way we can."

It was impossible to tell them apart: they seemed to be one person. And they too seemed to be aware of their oneness.

"We're familiar with computers."

"Well. Welcome to my frustration. I would be delighted if you can help me finish setting up these computers for this coming year's class." Father Wolfe waved a despairing hand in a large arc, indicating the frustrations. "And networking them."

As soon as they started to work, Father Wolfe realized he had here a God-send for his troubles. When he had started praying to St. Peter Canisius, whose *Catechism* had sold so well, for help in this correlative—correlative to St. Peter and himself—media venture, Xavier Carroll had appeared out of nowhere. And then Al Friedl was the man with the solutions. And now almost immediately after Father Al's breakdown, the brothers had stepped in. St. Peter was doing his stuff, all right.

With a few touches on the keys and in and out with programming disks, they casually wiped the old programs from the computers—everyone seemed to have his own way of setting up a network, or was it just Father Wolfe's inability to follow what was being done?—again installed Windows 98 and Word 97 programs. Not the latest word-processing software, but more than good enough to get the Pentiums in top shape for the in-class writing.

But when they came to the network, something still wasn't working right.

Exactly where Father Wolfe had stalled in each of his solo attempts.

"Father, your Novell network disk is not set up correctly..."

"...but we have just the one you need at home."

"Hiya, Father." It was Tony Santos. "You look wiped out, Old Priest." He said it as though it were a real title.

"Tony, you have come at precisely the right time. Do you have your Jeep here at school?" Luke didn't wait for an answer.

"We need some quick transportation for these two geniuses here." Father Wolfe smiled a delighted if tired smile at the look-a-likes. "Where do you live?"

"Five minutes."

"Third Avenue and Dromedary."

"Tony, could you take them home and bring them back?"

"Plenty of time, Father." And he grinned his big grin.

"OK, guys. Go with Tony. Please get what you need and bring it back now. Or, if you prefer, tomorrow when you come to class."

St. Peter Canisius, thank you.

"Father, why don't you come..."

"...with us? You'll probably like to see..."

"...our workshop."

How could he refuse them?

"Sure, come on, Father. I want to see it too." Tony was his usual engaging self.

The boys were right. Up John F. Kennedy Drive the quarter mile to Dromedary, left on Dromedary, then right on Third Avenue. A quarter of a block. It was a quiet tract house—all brick, one story, white trim—with a large and very neat yard. Grass—was it rye?—that was thick and green almost all over—an obvious feat in the midst of all the desert heat and lack of rain—but all the more applauded by the sad attempts at lawns in the neighboring houses to the right and the left.

This one was neatly framed in a pretty stretch of lantana. One stately fifty-foot palm, neatly trimmed. Two light-headed cottonwoods at the eastern edge of the property.

"Park in the street, Tony. Our dad comes..."

"...back in late afternoon in his truck and he likes..."

"...to park it in the driveway."

They walked back on the driveway along the side of the house, and there in the northeast corner of the back yard was a large, neat shed. White, newly painted. With a neat newly shingled roof.

Barry opened the door by punching the code numbers into the lock. Then as they entered, the brothers stepped back to usher in their two guests. Tony and Father Luke gasped as one. The whole thirty-by-thirty square room was awash with electronic equipment. There were computers, some running, some gutted—apparently to cannibalize parts. One in the corner with a Solitaire puzzle—only half-worked—on the screen—seemingly anxiously waiting to be conquered. Video cameras. Several bullhorns. A PA system. At least three VCRs. Two DVD players. Some fifteen speakers ringed the room. A three-foot-high robot—made apparently from glued- or wired-together Coke cans—was sitting on the table next to the door. The nose was a rubber pencil eraser, the eyes were kids' marbles with corneas painted in, and the ears were just holes in the proper places in the can that was the head. The mouth was a streak of black where mouths usually occur.

The aluminum man greeted them all in a high, squeaky Andy Devine voice. The tone resembled the flat articulation of automatic telephone answering devices. But higher—as though a rather intelligent English horn were offering its services.

"Howdy. Welcome to Mohr Electronics—the funnest place in the universe." And it made a welcoming—if awkward—palm-up gesture with its right hand.

"Thank you, Molly. That's just fine. And be..."

"...quiet now while we show Father and Tony around."

Molly obediently and abjectly brought her hand back down on her knee and tilted her head forward in seeming hurt dejection at this response to her usual routine.

"We call her Molly, because we modeled her after..."

"...our last year's religion teacher, Mrs. Molly Fied." Barry looked up at Father Wolfe, and the corner of his lip went up a little. "She wants her patronymic pronounced FEYE-yed, of course. But we irreverently say FEYED."

Where had they picked *patronymic* up?

Tony ran his hand over his shaved pate. And laughed. "Well, it does kinda look like her."

"We have all sorts of..."

"...other interesting things."

And an hour or so later, they were in the middle of showing how even the most sophisticated ears could not find the origin of the bullhorn's voice when it was bounced off eighteen-inches-wide yard-long sheets of Reynolds Wrap.

"Dad's home."

And there on one of the computer screens what looked like a two-and-a-half-ton Dodge truck with its massive grill was inching up the driveway.

"Father. Tony. We hafta run. Mom..."

"...wants us in for supper as soon as Dad..."

"...gets home. Here's the Novell disk you need, Father."

"We'll bring it tomorrow."

"Is there a copyright permissions problem here?"

"No, Father, when we bought it, we paid all the necessary fees to use..."

"...it however we liked."

"Man, those kids are really something, hunh, Father? With all my brilliance shown in your class"—Tony looked fleetingly askance at Father Wolfe as they drove back to Kino in the Jeep to see if he was enjoying the irony of Tony's often response of "I haven't a clue" to one of Father Wolfe's questions—"I could never begin to do what those two kids are doing." And he continued to bubble on and on in his amazement at what the brothers had wrought.

TWELVE

The next day as Father Luke was opening the classroom, Terry and Barry showed up with their Novell disk, and before the first summer session warning bell they had programmed all the computers to work together and print on the class' somewhat old but still efficient Laser 6P.

Thank you, St. Peter. Thank you for Xavier and Al and these wonderful kids. Thank you. Again.

THIRTEEN

"Father, we have to see you soon." Father Wolfe's mind was back from that pleasant reverie to the computer-problem solution of the summer before. But it was still Monday morning, March 23, Kino College Preparatory.

"About a very important matter." Terry frowned at Barry.

"But it's kinda personal." Barry glanced at Tony.

Tony laughed a little and took the hint. "Gotta catch the little lady, Father." And he headed for the stairs.

And the bell intruded itself again.

"Well, I can't right now, guys. That was the last bell. We have to start class now. After second period, at the beginning of Break?"

Terry looked at Barry, and Barry looked at Terry. This clearly was not what they had hoped for. "OK." The response came simultaneously from both sides.

Father Luke could almost hear the sigh of resignation.

Did Mr. and Mrs. Mohr intend that their triplets should have pun names? And Terry and Barry even pronounced their patronymic MORE. Had they been thinking when they had had them baptized Terence and Barry? And their sister was Mary?

Tony was back. "Here's Rita." A small girl, with very black hair and wearing a Mother Teresa's jumper over her white blouse, had suddenly materialized in front of Father Wolfe's desk.

When she smiled and looked the priest in the eyes, they shared their understanding about her turning Larry Curtland around—as Father Wolfe had hoped she would—from the boy's desire to kill all abortionists just as he thought he had killed his abortionist father. That had been two-three weeks ago. She was on the thin side but with the girl curves in all the right places. Without making a show of it, she leaned a little into Tony.

"Have you heard the good news?" Tony was smiling. "The Curtland kid wants to join Rita and me at daily Mass. What do you think about that?"

"I think it's terrific, Ton."

"And the neat thing about it all is that Larry is gonna be given God's help in his life in a special way, just like Rita and I have been experiencing."

It's as, *Tony,* as *when you want to compare with a following clause.*

"And God will keep him from making a move on my girl—as I was afraid he would do ever since I first saw that—well—adoration in his eyes."

Well, he got that one right.

"That's a selfish motive, Father. I know that. But I'm glad all the same."

Father Wolfe smiled. It was always refreshing to hear teenagers talk this way about God and themselves.

"Rita and I gotta go now, Father. Can't have Rita late for Mrs. Coulter's math. And I hafta be back for Bofford's Christian Commitment. It's very convenient that we both have the same free period." And they were no longer there.

FOURTEEN

And for a few moments Father Wolfe was back to yesterday—Sunday—morning. He had been standing just outside the main door of St. Ignatius Loyola church next door to Kino, in full vestments after the 9:00 o'clock Mass he had just said.

"Oh, Father Wolfe. You don't remember me." No, he did not. Neither voice nor face.

"I'm sorry. I'm not too good at remembering names."

"I'm Marie Goodwin." A stocky elderly woman who had a girlishly pretty and bright complexion on a classic English face with sculpted high cheeks. There was a shock of white on the left side of her otherwise black hair and the eyes of a woman who loved life. "My boys were Tim and Johnny. You had them in class twenty years ago. And I just wanted to say how much I appreciated your bringing Our Lady, the Blessed Virgin Mary, the Mother of our God, so strongly into your homily this morning." Marie Goodwin did not quite gush. But she spoke very quickly. "Somehow She seems to have been much forgotten." It was easy to tell from the inflection of her voice that she was mentally capitalizing the pronoun. "Not that She should take precedence over Jesus. But, as you said, it is through Mary that Jesus' graces come."

"Yes, Marie. We must never forget her or her place in our being called to the Father through Jesus." It was always a pleasure to hear old-line Catholics speak with such reverence for the Mother of God—they had learned well enough to pray to her in their greatest needs.

"And what are Tim and Johnny doing now?"

"Well, Tim is in the shipping business. He is an upper echelon manager for Barigold Import/Export in New York. And Johnny is teaching—English"—she smiled in recognition of the mutual joke: Johnny had done very poorly in Father Luke's class: he never seemed able to finish the assignments on time—"at Chief Oshkosh High School in Madison, Wisconsin. That's where he met his now-wife when they were both going to the University. Very much a Wisconsin girl."

She touched the white shock of hair with her left hand as though she wanted to be sure it was still there.

"And you and your husband are doing well?"

"Oh, Father, my Harry went to God five years ago."

"I'm sorry."

Marie went right on as though she had not heard him. "But I find that being a widow isn't that bad. For me anyway. My daughter Gina—Regina—she's Senator Wainwright's wife—has taken me into their home. And they take good care of me. So that I don't need much to live on. Neither of the boys is making that much money. But they send what they can afford now and then.

"But I'm not worried. When the Senator dies—if he precedes me, Gina will have his bank account. And if she dies before me, I am heavily into the millions in her will. Her uncle was the odd-ball-out of our family, Father. He made a bundle of money when the City of Chicago wanted the three acres of land on the lakeshore that he owned and was using as a marine sales and repair company—you may have heard of Henry Boats. The bundle of money he received he put into investments. And he got lucky. Very.

"And he thought my little Regina was the cutest little girl in the world. And so—eccentrically—when she was only six years old, he willed her everything he had. Exactly how much it came to, I'm not sure. But it must have been in the millions. The rest of the family he simply ignored. And then, ironically, in a boat accident two years later, he died, and all the money came to her. The attempts of the rest of the family to get at least some of it didn't stand up in court.

"And I have a part-time job as assistant librarian over there at St. Ignatius Grammar School." She did a half gesture and nodded her head in the direction of the one-story brick building—it was in the form of a box fifty yards long and twenty-five yards wide, with a patio in the center, several basketball courts on its east side and next to that a little kids' playground—guarded by at least ten happy ficus trees—with swings and things to climb on and through—one hundred yards to the east of the church. "And I help Gina in much of her charity work for the marginalized"—she paused as though that long and vague word took time to settle into both of their thought processors—"in our community."

FIFTEEN

"Mary, teach us to serve your Son with pizzazz." Father Luke was brought back to the Monday morning classroom by the typically male prayer after the class had said the *Hail Mary.* The sophomores shouted, "Amen," and sat down all together, like an oversized and uncoordinated dromedary. At the beginning of the year their *Amen* for an ending for prayer had been mumbled, half whispered. And then Father Wolfe had explained that the *Amen* had to be loud enough for God to hear. And the result was this much-enjoyed—to judge from the volume and smiles on their faces—stentorian shout.

"That was very good, Joel." Father Wolfe smiled at Joel Appleton, as he did every time he looked at the elfin nose on the clearly defined structure of his face under the wide-spaced blue eyes and short hair. "Even if it sounded rather familiar."

"My brother George said you liked it the other day when he used 'gusto' instead of 'pizzazz' in his senior class—when it was, like, his turn to lead the prayer."

"I did. Thank you."

"Words on the board, Marty?" Marty Johnson was the class secretary for vocabulary work. He had been staring out the window with his tiny black eyes squinched.

"Gary, please get going on the first five words." After the mild reproof, Marty had come alive.

"Father, can I have a marking pen?" It was Terry Mohr. Or was it Barry? Yes, it really was

Terry—Father Wolfe could see the congenital cleft in his left ear lobe. It was Barry's ears that were both normal. Terry now wore a worried look.

"The first word for next week, gentlemen"—Gary Gimble, looking as though his clothes (were they right side out?) were about to fall off him in another moment or two, so loose-jointed did he look under them, had written the first five words on the board and was dragging his words out now as though Father Wolfe were saying them and was trying to get the class to settle down—"is *zenith. Zenith* is a noun. It means the topmost point. The word comes from the Middle English and so there are no helpful roots in this word to aid our memories." He looked up at Father Wolfe on the other side of the classroom: he was clearly mimicking the priest's style of explanations. "And in our biography of St. Francis of Assisi, we read 'Only when Francis had reached the zenith of...'"

He gave a synonym for each word, explained their helpful roots and finally read the pertinent sentence in the biography of St. Francis Assisi—the Saint's life currently being used to exemplify the use of the vocabulary words.

Then Terry Mohr did the same for the second five words. After that Tyler Robertson in his mellow Deep South voice—where did he get it?—led them in reviewing last week's test.

"Father, was St. Francis a nerdy guy?" Michael Salvatierra looked up at Father from over his rimless glasses and under his long, lanky hair—did he ever wash it?—from his corner seat by the window.

"Why do you ask, Mike?"

"Well, if he was a sissy, he couldn't have been much of a Saint." A few snickers came from those around him. But most of the class had missed it.

"No, Mike." Father Wolfe laughed and looked out the window. "Assisi—the town he was from—had nothing to do with sissy." More laughter. Louder.

Hugh Nohs was at his parade marshal best when he ran the crossword puzzle for the week, choosing captains for each side of the class—the three window rows vs. the three door rows—and ushering Peter D'Amico up to the teacher's desk to offer synonyms of the words to be filled in in the puzzle he had created the night before.

As he sat in an empty student desk near the back of the room by the window, Fr. Luke's mind went back again to the night before. *What a beautiful and wonderful woman to be so brutally sent to you, Lord. She will be missed by many, many people. Lord Jesus, bring her—right now—to the full rich joy You have promised each of us in Your crucifixion.*

He was brought back to the class when Frank Baines, the human stopwatch for the contest, called time on Mike Feeney who was sitting directly behind Father Luke. In a stage whisper Mike said, "Aw, shit." A couple of snickers here and there. And everyone within four or five desks looked at Father Wolfe to see how he would take this.

"Guys. Hold everything." Each year for each class he gave the same speechlet when the situation, as it did now, made it seem more pertinent. "There are all sorts of words in our language like *shit* and *asshole* and all their kith and kin." There was a snicker here and there in the class. "But you never expect the President of the United States—whether you're a Democrat or Republican doesn't matter—or your favorite Sunday preacher to use them in a public speech. There's nothing wrong with these words, save that we have all tacitly agreed that they are not words for ordinary public consumption. *Shit*, for instance has all sorts of synonyms, all of which are perfectly acceptable—even though *shit* is not. *Detritus*, *excrement*, *fecal matter*, *guano*, *refuse*, *feces*—they are all just a congeries of letters that mean pretty much the same thing and are perfectly acceptable to use in that Presidential acceptance speech you will make in, say, forty years from now. If you want to talk about that sort of thing, of course. And people who use these unacceptables regularly show a remarkable lack of originality.

Peter and Joey and Conrad had correctly answered "habiliments" and "shibboleth" and "permeate" to their synonym clues when it was their turn.

And when it was Mike's turn again, the proffered synonym was "fear of rivalry" and its synonym from the words they had supposedly studied was of course "jealousy," and when Frank called time, Marty said, "Aw, fecal matter!" Snickers from all those in the immediate vicinity.

"Time for this week's test." Hugh Nohs was at his organizing best. Eric Jones passed them out as well as the Scantron sheets for their answers and set up the Scantron machine with the key to the correct answers.

And ten minutes later the raucous bell announced the end of the period.

And all the while the two triplets—who sat next to one another—were exchanging looks, but no words, and fidgeting.

"Now, Father, could we talk now?" It was Barry.

"Break would be better."

SIXTEEN

"Hey, Father, can we postpone the memory till tomorrow?" Aaron Bunting was at his persuasive best. Large, slit mouth—slightly parted—that opened up his whole face when he talked. Waiting for the answer. Down-to-his-ears fire-red hair. Just a soupçon of dimples. "I forgot to study it, Father."

The bell had rung. All the seniors in Monday's Period Two, led by Kevin Carter, said the *Hail Mary* together. His invocation "Mary, teach us today's memory" was followed by a shouted "Amen."

Father Wolfe looked at Aaron. "Why not just listen to the intrepid and gallant men who have the courage to speak out their homework? And then from their repetition of these familiar sounds you can learn it in five minutes.

"You want to recite the memory for us, Alex?"

It was memory day for this class of seniors. Alex Knowles—Marine Corps punctual on everything—extracted his six-foot-three-inch palm tree-trunk body out of his desk, smiled a knowing smile at Father Luke and the rest of the class and unhesitatingly monotoned,

"Death, be not proud, though some have
    called thee
Mighty and dreadful, for thou are not so;
For those whom thou think'st thou
    dost overthrow,
Die not, poor Death, nor yet canst thou kill me.
From rest and sleep, which but thy pictures be,

Much pleasure; then from thee much more
must flow.
And soonest our best men with thee do go,
Rest of their bones and soul's delivery.
Thou art slave to fate, chance, kings and
desperate men
And dost with poison, war, and sickness dwell.
And poppy or charms can make us sleep as well
And better than thy stroke; why swell'st
thou then?
One short sleep past, we wake eternally
And death shall be no more; Death, thou shalt die."

Father Luke wrote in an *A* in the proper space in Alex's marking-book line. "Excellent, Alex. John Donne would have been delighted to hear his masterpiece done so well."

And without you, Jesus, Death would have had the final say for Gina.

"Father." It was Francisco Morales with the inevitable question. "Are you punning on John Donne's name?"

"Why not? He did it himself all the way through his 'Hymn to God the Father.'"

"Father, doesn't John Donne know that Alex recited well? You said he would have been delighted." That was Chris Summers over by the door.

Francisco had questions about everything. And he was often abetted by Chris in his attempts to sidetrack the class. But how else do we learn? "Doesn't he hear him if he is in heaven—or—umm—wherever else he might be?"

"Right on, Paco." How the Spanish language got from *Francisco* to *Paco* was an ever-mystery to Father Wolfe. "We certainly hope John made it to the joy of God's presence and is clapping his hands for Alex right now.

"Adam?"

"I'm not prepared, Father." Adam reached up and grabbed his left ear in embarrassment. And only half got out of his desk.

And immediately Father Luke was back in the freezer of last night. He too certainly had not been prepared for the sight of that mannequin corpse. Of the brutal destruction and pain that Death had wrought. It certainly looked as though Death had been proud. His handiwork had been mighty and dreadful.

Jesus, bring that wonderful woman to Yourself. Now. She was so full of life and love for others here. Bring her to Your full, rich joy You plan for all of us.

Father Wolfe looked up sadly at Adam, sighed and wrote in an *F* next to Adam Checkles'—he pronounced it SHECK-lees—name.

He had had no idea whom Death's handiwork had destroyed until the police started to remove the corpse from the freezer. And suddenly—did he gasp again?—he recognized Gina Wainwright, the senator's wife and the mother of Benjy, a sophomore in his first-period class.

And when it came to Aaron Bunting's turn near the very end, he had managed to learn those fourteen lines with an *um* and an *oh* here and there.

They had all finished. Father Wolfe closed his marking book. "'Sonnet 4' for next week, gentlemen.

'At the round earth's imagined corners....' It's the next poem in the lit book. Another John Donne classic.

"OK, guys. Let's look at *Othello.* Where did we leave off yesterday?

"Friday, Father. Yesterday was Sunday."

Getting old really ain't for sissies.

"OK. Where did we leave off Friday?"

"Father, why do we have to memorize all these poems?" It was Francisco again. "We'll never use them. Or even see them." It was almost a little kid's whine.

"Well, Paco, I would have hoped by now that you would have ceased to be such a philistine as to think that nothing had value unless it had some practical use, brought about some material profit."

"What's a philistine, Father?" That was Paulino Hernandes this time. Paulino with his bushy sideburns down to below the bottom of his ears. Paulino loved to stall the class as much as possible. Even more than Aaron or Chris did.

"Why not look it up in the handy pocket-sized dictionary in the file cabinet? You could add a nice, new word to your vocabulary."

"Pretty big pocket, Father. That book is two feet by a foot-and-a-half and ten inches thick." And he got up and headed for the file cabinet in the back corner away from the windows.

"How can you come to experience the richest expressions of the human condition in our language if you do not advert to them and try to make them your own?"

Am I being too schoolmarmish?

"How about Act II, Scene 1, Line 158?" He looked around the classroom. "Everybody got it?

"Mark, remind us. Why does Iago hate Othello?"

Mark Miller always seemed about to disappear into his desk by some kind of magic act whenever he was called on. "Well, you see, Iago thought he should have been given the job Cassio had gotten." His voice was almost inaudible. "Othello's aide de—um—camp."

"Any other reason, Justin?"

Justin Bell sat next to the window and was at the moment fascinated by a mourning dove's activities on the lawn outside. "Father?"

"Did Iago have any other reason to hate Othello?"

The answer seemed dredged out of a deep, viscous swamp. "Kinda."

"You wouldn't care to explain, would you?"

"Sarcasm, no sarcasm, Father." That was Alex Knowles. In spite of his usual retiring manner, he had picked up from his friend Greg Farrell, who, in Father Luke's other senior class, had taken it on himself since the beginning of the year to be Father Luke's conscience when it came to turning hurtful corners with his comments. And since Greg had enjoyed it so much, Alex Knowles decided to take over the job in this class.

"All right. How about: Do you want to add to that, Ricky?"

Ricky Shipley sat by the windows in the last row. Answers usually had to be pried from him. Even if he was probably the brightest in the class. "Well, he said he *kinda*—with the meaningful emphasis, he smiled a little around his small mouth and from behind his oversize glasses—"lusted after her. Kinda. And he said that maybe he should even have gotten Othello's job as Commander-in-chief."

"Excellent, Ricky."

Ricky owlishly looked around to see if the others had appreciated Father's compliment.

"Let's roll it—where Iago says to Desdemona, 'To suckle fools and chronicle small beer.' Do you want to take that, Brad, and tell us what Iago is saying?"

"Well, um, I think he seems to be saying..." Bradley Allen was at his disingenuous best, trying to get the class' sympathy and goad Father Wolfe into calling on someone else for a clear-cut answer to a conundrum in this seemingly ancient language of William Shakespeare. Father Wolfe's obvious goal in these line-by-line questions was to help the students find in William's works very modern ideas, even if the language was somewhat difficult to get used to.

"Brad, we're not really interested in what Iago seems to be saying." Father Wolfe smiled and changed his copy of *Othello* from one hand to the other. "And we are not really interested in what you think about this right now—however wise your opinion and much to be cherished by all mankind."

"Sarcasm, Father. No sarcasm." It was Alex Knowles again.

"We want to know what he *is* saying."

"He is saying that women are not much good for anything except to bring children into the world and make non-alcoholic beer."

Much to Brad's surprise, the class as one erupted in an explosion of laughter.

"Well, I suppose that is a possible meaning of *small*."

Suddenly the merciful bell rang.

SEVENTEEN

Before the seniors had all filed out, Terry and Barry were there.

"Father, we really have something we really hafta talk to you about." The repetition underscored the anxiety in their eyes.

"You must promise us that you will never even breathe what we tell you to a soul." That was Terry. He didn't wait for Father Wolfe's commitment to his demand. But he bubbled on, apparently urged on by the need to let the whole world know. "You see, last night, around one o'clock, me and Barry—uh, Barry and I"—Terry glanced at Father Luke and then looked long at Barry—"um, liberated our father's truck to go driving around the city while he was asleep."

"Neither one of us have driver licenses, Father." Barry lowered his head and looked up with only his eyes to see how Father Wolfe was taking this.

"And so we hadda slip the keys off the hook in the kitchen where Dad always leaves them after work. This way we could joyride his truck around town for a coupla hours. And no one would know the difference."

Well, they can talk in complete sentences, after all.

"He drives one of those refrigerator trucks around the Valley to deliver food to people's houses."

"You know. Ice cream. Frozen meat. Super-cooled veggies."

"You have seen the truck." That was Barry.

"You have, Father. Last summer at our house when our father came home. It's a two-and-a-half-ton Dodge with a big *Schwartz's…*"

"…in bright-red letters…"

"…on each side and on the back of his refrigerated truck. Refrigerated: that's important."

"Big letters."

"Well, we started off by opening the freezer box in back and getting a popsicle—you know, one of those frozen sugar things on a stick—for each of us."

Do I look so old that I do not know what a popsicle is?

"And then we drove around for an hour or so..."

"...and saw this basketball sitting on the ground under the—um—east basket of Riordan Playground..."

"...you know, the park over at Seventh Street and Mountain." Terry tugged at his left ear.

"So we got out and, like, bucketed a few. Then Terry"—Barry quickly glanced at his brother—"wanted to stop at an all-night QT for a frozen Snickers.

"And then I reminded him that we had a whole truck full of frozen Snickers bars. Well, not a whole truckful, but a lot. And so we..."

"...opened the back door of the truck again, the freezer box."

"It was closed but unlocked."

"Something our father just never did."

"Leave it unlocked, that is."

"Something we had not thought of when we went for the popsicles."

"And this time found this body."

"It was all covered with blood..."

"...and frozen as stiff as a–um–popsicle." Terry bit his lip as he looked up at Father Wolfe's face.

EIGHTEEN

"We hate to admit it, Father..."

"...but we were both scared out of our minds." Barry nodded in agreement.

"No idea what to do with it. Didn't know how it got there."

"It hadn't been there..."

"...when we got the popsicles."

"It was clear we must have left the door open when we got the popsicles out."

"And so we couldn't tell our father. He'd be very upset to find a corpse in his truck. And he would of course suspect us..."

Yes, he certainly would. And so would the police: who else had access to the truck keys?

"...not of having murdered someone. But somehow."

Be careful of that story, Luke. Is there something awry here?

"We have been known—um—to play pranks on him and our sister–the one that's the other one-third of the triplets." Barry scarcely glanced at Father.

"So we couldn't just leave it there. And we didn't know..."

"...what to do with it."

"It's a human body. And if she was Catholic..."

"...she should be buried after..."

"...a funeral Mass in a Catholic church."

"And no matter what her religion..."

"...she deserves some kind of a decent burial."

"And then, Terry"—Barry glanced at his brother again—"remembered that you guys—uh—you priests have a walk-in freezer..."

"...in your kitchen. And if we could leave the..."

"...body there, you priests would know what..."

"...to do with it. Know what to do about it..."

"...and treat it with respect. And..."

"...make sure it got properly prayed over."

"And then you'd tell the police."

"We knew the layout because..."

"...we both work there often..."

"...washing dishes..."

"...you know, to help pay our tuition."

"Yes. But you guys couldn't get in. Father Friedl locks the place up like a bank every night."

"Well..." Barry looked uncomfortably at his brother.

"...one evening when Barry was taking the trash out after we had cleaned up, he discovered that even when you close the back door and think the latch has locked—you can even hear the click—it never completely closes. And the garden gate has a lock on it that fits wrong so that you can open it by just lifting the gate a little."

"But how did you get through the outer gate into the parking lot?"

Larry looked helplessly at his brother again. "Well, we knew that if..."

"...you applied just the right pressure on the opening side of the sliding gate—we learned this one night when..."

"...Harry Plotter came late for football practice and the gate was locked and he couldn't get in and we were right behind him in Benjy's—Benjy Wainright's—Mustang and wanted to watch the practice."

"And so now we don't know what to do."

"Did your father take the truck out this morning?"

"We suppose so, Father. We always hafta leave earlier than he gets going. We carpool with Norm Balinski. You know him."

"He's in one of your classes. The guy with the big glasses and..."

"...the semi-truck horn voice." Barry gestured toward his throat and his own inability to have one so notable.

They were both clearly accurate reporters.

The PA voiced its insistence that Break was over.

"Well, look, guys, we have to phone and tell your father about this and then the police. This is probably murder. Does your father have a cell-phone?" Father Wolfe walked from the door to his desk and picked up his phone and turned to repeat his question to Barry and Terry. But they had evaporated.

Students were flooding by. Luke quickly moved to the doorway and stopped the first one he knew, Louis Franklin who was in his second senior class.

"Louie, you know the Mohr brothers, don't you?" Louis would find them if anyone could.

"Sure, Father. Everybody does—even if we don't know which one is which." He laughed.

"Well, run out there into the hall and see if you can find them and bring them back."

"May I talk to Captain Oscar Parsons? Father Wolfe had checked his date/address/phone-number book and had dialed the city jail. "Yes, tell him Father Wolfe is calling." In a few words he brought the Captain up to date on what the two boys had told him.

"Thank you, Father. We'll see how we can make all this fit together."

Louie Franklin was back. "No way, Father. I couldn't find them. And no one I asked had seen them."

NINETEEN

"Morning, Father." It was Father Luke's prep period. Still Monday, the twenty-third. Just before lunch. "How've you bin? I haven't seen you around for a while." John Finney was at his best—as to hair and as to saying exactly what he thought: almost completely bald and jovial.

Father Luke laughed. It was always a pleasure to meet John. That, in spite of his penchant for warmed-over stories that inevitably involved a pun. With that exception, he was always optimistic and happy and gregarious.

"Busy, I guess." Father Luke made a move toward the teachers' computer lab in the next room.

"Do you have Benjamin—well, everyone, including himself, calls him Benjy—Wainright in class?"

"Yes, I do. Nice kid."

"That's part of the irony, Father, He is a nice kid. But I really worry about him."

"Because?"

"Well, as you know, Father, I live with my Mary and our Horace and Matilda"—some people still did give their children those old-fashioned names—"up there off upper John F. Kennedy."

It was part of John's charm that he innocently enough liked himself to be known as one who hob-nobbed with the socially or—to put it another way—moneyed elite. Most would have said *northern* John F. Kennedy Drive. But John was the only one that Father knew who said *upper*—obviously to stress the fact that he lived in a tony neighborhood. They had lived on a much more modest street to the northeast of the school on John's teacher salary. But his Mary had won several hundred thousand buckeroos—as John called them—in a lottery of some sort, and they had decided—after they had put enough away for their children's college tuition and expenses–to give a sizable chunk to a poor priest in Nicaragua John had heard about. Finally, they had moved to a "nicer"—as John wanted it known—neighborhood.

"Well, the Senator, for all of his idiosyncrasies is basically a generous guy. I'm sure some of this has to do with getting the vote. But he often enough simply opens his house to his neighbors. And that's us. One neighbor family anyway."

"But why does that make you worry about Benjy?" Sometimes it was difficult to keep John on track. Was this an "idiosyncrasy" his classes suffered in silence?

"There is this guy, an abortion doctor, Aldo Bier, who lives in the same neighborhood and is also often invited to these get-togethers. And Benjy is of course there. And this guy keeps making a big play for Gina, the Senator's wife."

Doesn't he know she's been murdered?

"She's graciously friendly with absolutely everyone. But this guy Bier is really taken with her kindness. And makes no secret of it. Bringing her coffee or cake or whatever they are having—even before she needs it. And holding her hand. And looking at her unabashedly—this, even though his wife Emily is right there in the same room and is watching the whole circus—with a disgusted smile on her face. I guess that's the best way to put it, Father. And Emily's no scarecrow herself, Father. The doctor is obviously making some kind of play for Gina.

"What's with all these abortion doctors? Don't they stop at murder? Are they all lechers, too?"

Father Wolfe wondered if he should point out the fallacy of *ab uno disce omnes*—judge everyone from what just one does—but perhaps at a later date. And while he's at it, to point out the reverse order of gravity for the sins.

How do I stop him long enough to tell him what's happened?

"And Benjy is there to watch all this—the good Senator wanting the whole family present at these public gatherings to foster his wholesome image.

"You can imagine the effect this has on Benjy. Whenever he is there at one of these parties, he seems sad—just the opposite of the used-to-be happy kid you and I have in class. I think that's why he has changed.

"The Senator sees it, too. And he is not pleased, obviously. But he seems to have done nothing about it."

"Well, thank you for telling me." There seems no point in trying to tell him about her death now. He will find out soon enough. "I'll try to be kinder to Benjy. Perhaps he will decide to want to talk about this. And then I'll try to help you help him. If we can."

"Kinda like that Doctor Brandt and my Mary. Remember? I told you about that three, four weeks or so ago. But my Mary in blunt Angular-Saxon terms told him to get lost. But this Gina seems to think that she can be kind and smile and loving to just everybody in the same way." Does he really think *angular* is the right word? Or is this just one of his puns, this time on *Anglo*? John scratched his not-too-well-shaven throat. That was the signal as all the teachers at Kino knew that they were about to be pun-ished by one of John's stories.

Well, at least they aren't double entendres.

"Father, did I ever tell you about the orange juice manufacturer who refused to will his business to his son who did poorly in school?" These jokes seemed to be the denouement of every conversation with him.

Father Wolfe knew the answer to this one. The whole faculty knew. He was tempted to tell John. But why hurt this wonderful man?

"He figgered that if he had never learned to concentrate he could never run an orange juice factory." And John snuffled. "Gotta catch Amy Bates about my appointment tomorrow with Father Sloan. Good talking to you." And he was out the door.

TWENTY

Father Wolfe had hardly unlocked and opened the classroom door after lunch when Harry Smathers as if on cue materialized out of no particular place. It was Monday afternoon. And Father Luke could think only of a bliss-filled siesta as soon as the last class had gone.

"Father Wolfe, good afternoon."

"Harry, how are you this fine Kino afternoon?" There was something particularly pleasant about the way Harry Smathers wore his African-American self as a cheerful badge of who he was. He was somehow always happy and surprisingly self-assured for a seventeen-year-old. And that always made it fun to tease him. "Is the greatest English scholar in the whole world ready for class?"

"Well, we'll have to find out about that today when Greg Farrell rules: he'll likely call on me just to show me he knows more about lidrudchuh"—he smiled and said the word as he supposed the Prime Minister of England would—"than I do. But tomorrow—oh, we don't meet tomorrow, do we? Wednesday I will be the greatest English scholar ever, Father. That's when under my astute leadership I lead the exhilarated class in a Socratic dialogue to determine the great depths of meaning, the aesthetic reverberations and the gentle music of Rudyard Kipling's 'Gunga Din.'"

Father Wolfe laughed. Greg and Harry's facsimile rivalry was one of the fun parts of the class.

"And that's when I will remind the class of what Johnny Pitts came up with when he saw this poem on your list for our choices a couple of months back."

"Which was?"

"'He asked, "Do you like Kipling?" And she said, "I don't know: I've never kippled."'"And then came the non-sequitur: "How do you like my new shirt?"

Father put his cup of iced tea from lunch down on his desk and took a better look at Harry. On the front of his black T-shirt in three-inch-high white letters was: "FRONT."

"Well, that figures. It's on your front side as you're wearing it."

"Whoa. Wait. You are only half-finished with your examination." And he turned around. And on the back—the white half of his T-shirt—in the same Times New Roman three-inch-high black letters was: "BACK." And in the space between the *B* and the *A* sat a caret. And there above the two letters on either side was a large scrawled *L*. "Think everyone will be jealous?"

Father Wolfe laughed. "I love it."

"I thought you'd like it. All you English teachers have a thing for words."

"Has the Dean seen it yet?"

"I know it doesn't have a collar, Father, but right now I'm gonna parade right by him with this shirt untucked to see what he says. Maybe the untucked part of things will make him just a little bit jealous of this little old shirt and distract him from his no-collar fixation. And, like, I hope all the other seniors will be jealous of little old me, too."

It was *envious*, of course, of what you want—*jealous* of what you have. But now was not the time to remind him of what they had taken in class just this past week.

"Good luck."

"I just wanted to be sure you saw it before—maybe he'll trash it."

"He'll probably just laugh and ignore the rule. You got away with a similar one a couple of weeks ago."

"I hope it'll be a repeat."

TWENTY-ONE

"Harry, would you like to tell the class the meaning of the next four lines?" It was fifth period, right after lunch, and Greg Farrell—the excellent student since his "conversion," as he explained it, due to his having fallen in love with a Mother Teresa girl and now wanting to be the best man he could be for the new light in his life—was at the lectern at the front of the class, taking his turn at Socratically helping the class unravel the poem he had chosen from the list of titles Father Luke had given them earlier in the semester. Just before, the class in quick order had recited "Death, be not proud." And now under Greg's questioning were very much into explicating Browning's "My Last Duchess."

"You mean lines—umm—thirty-one, thirty–two, thirty-three and thirty-four?" Harry was still wearing his loud T-shirt. Was the Dean beginning to relax on his regulations toward the end of the school year?

"Those are the next four, Harry."

"Greg, no sarcasm. Remember?" Larry Curtland was smiling like a fey Irish leprechaun as he said it. The class thought it was fun. And Father Wolfe apparently did too. It had been a given for months that Greg was the one in this class to correct Father Luke's insistence that there was to be no ironic comment about apparent stupidity. And Larry had taken it into his head to be Greg's stand-in while Greg ran the show.

"Harry, on with it. Read the next four lines for us." Greg might well make a great teacher someday.

He had the air of knowing all the answers and only hoping that his students would come to see what he saw.

"Okay.

> "She thanked men—good! but thanked,
> Somehow—I know not how—as if she ranked
> My gift of a nine-hundred-years-old name
> With anybody's gift."

"Yes. Now what does it mean?"

"Well." Harry rubbed his right palm across his nose. "The old Duke thinks that all these other guys—the gardener, the os—the ostler...." Harry turned around to Father Luke who was sitting in the back of the classroom. "Is that the right word, Father?"

"Right on, Harry. The stable hand. That's *hostler*, spelled with an *h* that most people do not pronounce."

"The stable hand. And the guy who was painting her portrait. The Duchess is giving them all the bright smile and gracious gift of her loving personality that embraced everyone. Just what Jesus wants."

Greg smiled. "That was a mouthful, Harry. But what was so wrong about that?"

"Well, nothing. Really."

"Except the Duke thought she was flirting with all these guys?"

"Not really." Harry rubbed his nose again. "The old Duke thought she should be paying more attention to his gifts than these other guys' gifts."

"And the best gift?"

"Yeah. That's weird, isn't it? A family name that's been around for nine hundred years. Like, Smathers back there in 1103 or so. Like maybe hobnobbing with ole Henry II—wasn't he the guy that deep-sixed Becket? Who cares how long a patronymic lives?" He turned around to grin at Father Wolfe. "Nice word, hunh, Father? Did I use it correctly?"

"Right on, Harry. Just the way a sophomore surprisingly used it yesterday."

"Sarcasm, Father. Sarcasm." Larry was enjoying doing Greg's job.

"Who cares how long a name has been in the family?" And he smiled again, this time at Greg up in front.

"Well, then. What was his problem?"

Harry could happily shout out the word that kept coming up in their line-by-line reading of *Othello*. "Jealousy."

"Very good, Greg. And Harry." Father Luke had gotten up and was walking up to the front of the class. "We'll finish off 'My Last Duchess' tomorrow. And now we'll go back to our *Othello*."

"Beadle Curtland, where are we?" It was Larry's job to be the super-secretary for this class.

"Act Three, Scene Two, Line 37. Where Othello is taking it from Iago. And is slowly beginning to doubt his wife's integrity."

"Pete, you're Iago. Mark, you're Othello. Roll it."

"Father, you said this was a male play. You don't mean to say that it's just us males who get jealous."

That was Angelo in his persona that loved to interrupt this class with his questions.

"That's *we*, Angelo. *It* is the dummy subject and *we* is the real subject and *males* is a restrictive appositive to *we*."

"Whatever."

"No, not whatever. *We* is the subject!"

"Whew. OK, Father, OK."

"What's so mysterious?" Father Wolfe relaxed.

Am I too pedantic about these petty matters?

"You guys learned all that stuff when you were freshmen and sophomores, didn't you?"

"Ummm. Supposed to, Father. Yeah, roll it, guys." Angelo was obviously trying to imitate Father Wolfe.

"No. Let me explain about jealousy. Women can be and often are jealous too. But males, caught in its web, often take things to wild extremes. What you read in the papers often enough is the man who comes home to find another guy in bed with his wife and pulls out the old ten-gauge and seriously ventilates first the other guy, then his wife, then his kids and then himself. Senseless. And you don't find a woman acting hers out so wildly. At least not usually. That's what I meant when I told you it was a male play. Jealousy. OK, Angelo?"

"Gotcha, Father."

"Roll it, guys."

"'Doubt?'" Mark Oberman was doing a very good job of adding incredulity to his voice.

And the PA's pseudo-bell rang.

TWENTY-TWO

"Well, good afternoon, Father. My name is Dr. Aldo Bier." The smile was deep and warm and friendly and manly. "I'm sorry I had to schedule this right after school today. But, you see, Mondays are a particularly busy day for me. And I had to rush over here to see as many of Bruno's teachers as I can today—the school year is so quickly coming to an end." Dr. Aldo Bier was the picture of success. A neat lightweight grey suit embracing a blue shirt and a brightly figured tie. "May I sit down?"

Father Wolfe expected him to pull out a fine cambric handkerchief and dust off the student-desk chair. "Certainly, Doctor."

"As I explained on the phone, and as you know, my son Bruno is in your class. Our whole family is Catholic, Father, and I am sending Bruno to Kino because I want him to have a good solid Catholic education. And a Jesuit one as well. I graduated from Borgia High School in Trenton, Father, and so I can appreciate the good things you people do.

"I really wanted you to know some of his background. His changing schools at the near end of the school year will, I am afraid, not only affect his marks but prejudice his ability to learn and progress the way he should.

"We're from Dallas, Father. And I know ah should be tawkin' with a drawl." The doctor flashed his handsome I-know-you-will-understand smile. But we haven't been living there long. My particular talent has moved me around the country."

"What is that talent, Doctor? Are you a surgeon, perhaps?" Father Wolfe somehow found it difficult to relax with this man.

"Why, yes, Father. How did you guess it? I specialize in freeing women from their burdens."

"And what kind of a surgeon is that, Doctor?"

"Why, an abortion provider, Father." He steepled his long graceful fingers into an imitation of praying hands. And smiled in a pleasant way that indicated he was sure that Father understood.

"Family Freedom urged me to come from a Dallas Freedom house to here. We had three doctors at our clinic in Dallas. And you people here in Phoenix have just lost both of your doctors at your clinic. Didn't one kill the other?"

Your clinic? What part belongs to me?

"Yes." Father Wolfe found it very difficult to keep his face placid and friendly and fatherly. He suppressed his desire to laugh sardonically. To snarl.

"And since we are Catholic, I wanted my Bruno to come to the best religious education possible."

Why? Lord, help this guy to get his act together. Catholic and murderer. Do apples grow on orange trees?

"Bruno went to your Jesuit high school in Dallas. And he was a good student. But his marks did not come easily. And I wanted to be sure all of you here would give him whatever benefit of the doubt you can because of his change of school."

"You can depend on that from me, Doctor." Father Wolfe suppressed the choking he felt in his throat.

"How is Bruno doing, Father?"

"Well, he has been here only two weeks, Doctor. But he works hard, and he seems to have picked up the aggressive approach to learning that we foster here."

"I'm glad to hear that, Father. Is there something I can do to help him succeed?"

"He seems to be having trouble with his reading, Doctor"—how hard it was to address that word to this man—"but one of the best things you—you or his mother—can do for him is to read the next book with him."

"That presents a problem, Father. His mother walked out on us—no goodbye; no suitcase; just our Ford Explorer—right before we left Dallas."

Little wonder. But rough on Bruno.

Doctor Bier studiously stared at his long-fingered palm-up hands in front of him. "And I have not been able to ascertain her whereabouts or contact her in any way. I even hired a private detective. And I"—Doctor Bier with the innocence of a four-year-old, looked up into Father Wolfe's eyes—"as you might suspect, am so overburdened by my profession that I have scarcely time to eat—much less read a book. As much as I would like to help him. Is there anything else I can do?"

"Doctor, you puzzle me." Father Wolfe knew it was a non-sequitur, but his anger was making him aggressive.

"Why is that, Father?"

"You say you are a Catholic. But the Church from day one has always insisted that abortion is evil, wrong, a huge sin. How do you manage to still call yourself a Catholic and at the same time jettison the most basic of moral rights: the right to life?"

Luke, Luke, don't let your anger take charge.

"Oh, Father, the Church has come a long way in 2000 years. And those of us involved Catholics who are on the cutting edge of the moral order applauded by Vatican II are rewriting the antique book of what's right and wrong. The world is changing. We must change with it. Wasn't it Sartre who said the end justifies the means? The end here is the woman's freedom. The means: take the burden from her."

"I don't know if Sartre said that. But way before his time, St. Ignatius and his Jesuits were insisting on it as a basic principle—with the condition that the end and the means be good, or at least indifferent. That is, not worthless. But neutral, certainly not evil."

"Ummm."

"But how can you reconcile the taking of a human life—no matter the reason or state it's in—with the Church's ever-insistence, before and after Vatican II, that human life is sacred?" Father Wolfe suddenly realized that he was very angry. "Have you personally read the official statements of Vatican II? Or Pope John Paul's *Veritatis Splendor*?" His voice was rising. His throat was constricting. He was getting angry.

"Well, no, I haven't, Father. But you don't really believe those stray bits of primordial tissue are human, do you?"

"What are they, then? The beginning of a rhinoceros?"

The doctor laughed an engaging laugh.

"Where do all the wonders that constitute a human being get suddenly added on to the very beginnings? Where else can they be unless everything is there from the very first moment?"

"Sorry if have expressed myself badly, Father. But I am sure that our ideas are really the same."

Is this guy slow, or have I *expressed myself badly? Didn't he say he went to a Jesuit high school? What happened to him after that? Or was his attention someplace else during the Catholic Morality class?*

"You see, Father, we both agree at the roots of things. But, I see, Father, that you have a very old-fashioned mind about life and the Church and the medical profession." He was rising from the student desk facing Father Wolfe's.

"I'm afraid I do, Doctor. Human life is the most basic gift we have from God. No life, no nada."

"I hope this won't hurt my Bruno's chances here, Father."

"Actually, it will probably help him."

As we pity this boy who finds himself in this incredible bind.

He expected the Doctor to ask why. But he was no longer in the room. His going had been graceful. And he had been smiling.

TWENTY-THREE

As he climbed into bed and told God he was sorry for his sins and asked Him to protect him through the night, Father Wolfe was sure that he would be gone in an instant. Monday had been an exhausting day. Instead, clear and sharp in his mind was the surprising experience of—when was that? Two weeks ago? Three? Forget sleep. With Yogi Berra, it was déjà vu all over again.

It had been first period. Tuesday. Second in the day—starting at 9:15—on the revolving schedule. So difficult to work with, it seemed, yet so simple to see on the bulletin board of his mind's eye:

Mon	Tues	Wed	Thurs	Fri
1	6	5	4	3
2	1	6	5	4
BREAK				
3	2	1	6	5
4	3	2	1	6
LUNCH				
5	4	3	2	

Its advantage, of course, is that it removes one source of student boredom: many teachers do not have a given class at the same time during the week. And so students have to keep alive to the daily change to make sure they arrive at the right class at the right time.

The sophomores hadn't eaten for almost an hour—*sarcasm, Father, no sarcasm*—and they were engaged in their most distasteful study: sentence structure.

"You want to tell us all about number twelve, David?" They were reviewing last week's test, and David Benter was so much the bright sober-sides boy that nobody ever seemed to call him by the diminutive Dave.

"Sure, Father. '...they saw that there was some bread there and a charcoal fire with fish cooking on it. ...that there was some bread there....' Is that the one you want me to do?"

"Is that the next one?"

"Uh, yes."

"Then, why not do it?"

"Sarcasm, Father. You always tell us never to be sarcastic." That was Skye—he had the simple smile of a happy child on a face that God seemed to have carved out with an ax—high cheek bones on a thin face with astonishingly black eyes set a little far apart. "Oh, I should have raised my hand." And he raised his hand.

"You're right, Skye. You seem to have taken over that job here from your senior cousin. Isn't Greg Farrell some kind of a distant relative?"

"No, Father. But he carpools me to school every day. And he often tells me how much fun he has correcting you."

"Umm. Well, on with the sentence, David."

"Well, *was* is a verb, so this must be a clause."

"Excellent, David. Now what kind of a clause is it? Sean—" Sean sat on the other side of the classroom, behind Father Luke's back as he stood in the middle of the class with its horseshoe-shaped seating—"and what kinds of clauses are there?"

"Uh, when, where, why—um...."

"Those are the adverbial questions, Sean." Sean had probably been talking to his neighbor, Matt Singleton. "Clauses. Remember? There are four and only four kinds of clauses. What are they?"

"There's a lady at the door, Father."

"That's not a kind of clause, Sean. You're trying to distract me. The four kinds of clauses?"

"But, Father, there *is* a lady at the door." Was this déjà vu from two weeks ago when both Mrs. Curtland—the wife of the murdered abortion doctor—and Lyda Lott—the TV reporter—had insisted on interrupting his class?

Father Wolfe turned to the open doorway and walked to meet the woman who really was there. Why did people think it was the most natural thing in the world to interrupt a class? Had all of their schooling been so dull that they welcomed any kind of distraction?

Her voice was very low, so low that Father Luke could scarcely hear her. "Father, I must talk to you. Now. My son Benjy—oh, I should introduce myself: I am Gina Wainwright, Senator Wainwright's wife—says that you can solve any problem." She was a beautiful woman. Fair. Light fluffy blonde hair. High cheekbones. Deep blue eyes—that she brought up to Father's and then looked down again. And still svelte. No wonder that the Senator loved to show her off by his side at every public appearance.

"Well, Mrs. Wainwright"—Father Luke was trying to be gentle—"we were just about to start our weekly quiz. And as soon as that's over, the period will end and the tykes will head out to lunch and then we can talk. Ten minutes. Will that be soon enough?"

"Yes, Father. I don't want to disturb anything, but I must see you." She was visibly upset.

"All right, guys, everything off the desk. Billy, will you please pass out the test in the copy machine's output trough? Danny, the Scantrons are on my desk. Please pass them out. Phil, please put the key—it's lying on top of my computer monitor—in the starting trough of the Scantron machine."

Five minutes later, one by one each student began to go to the Scantron machine—the sophisticated correcting device—to run his fill-in-the-bubble answer paper to see how well—or poorly—he had done on the test. For every mistake on a test the machine made a popping sound. When Jack Healy ran his through, the mechanical corrector sounded as though it were making enough popcorn to feed a whole theater. And the whole class—even the students still trying to concentrate at their desks—laughed quietly—aware that the answers of those yet to finish might produce an even greater supply of popcorn.

And the bell rang.

When the students had all left the classroom with their books and John Cotton had asked about the clause he had found so tricky, Gina Wainwright and Father Wolfe sat down by the window in student desks he had turned to face each other.

TWENTY-FOUR

"Father, I'm so frightened." There was no need for her to say that: fear was a monsoon blowing in from the southwest in those bright, blue eyes. "And I don't know what to do."

The smell of Fred's hamburgers waiting for Father Wolfe in the basement dining room of the faculty house momentarily bothered his nostalgic nose. He straightened the few white hairs on his head.

"My husband wants me to get an abortion. And I know I just can't do that. It's so wrong."

"You're right. It's murder."

"He says it's not his child." She stifled a sob that seemed to come from deep within her. "And I don't know what he's talking about. Whose would it be? He says I have been unfaithful to him. And, Father, that's just not true." Her sob now was brief, deep and constricted.

"It's OK to cry, Mrs. Wainwright. Is there some reason why he might think that was the case?"

Be delicate, Luke. Be delicate.

"Oh, Father." The tears had welled up, and she was dabbing at them with her handkerchief. "I try to be friendly and affectionate to everyone we meet. Because, well, I like people." And she smiled a slight smile, almost apologetic. "And to further my husband's chances for the governorship he longs for. But it has never gotten beyond that—no matter what anyone might say. But whatever my failings, Father, I have never"—and just from the way she said that *never*, it was clear that this was the truth—"been unfaithful to him in any way."

And Father Luke's memory segued back to the day he had given the seniors a list of the possible poems they would help the class explicate. And Greg Farrell had chosen Browning's "My Last Duchess." Under his excellent tutelage they would continue to endeavor—begun with today's effort—to understand on each of its levels this magnificent poem. The Duchess who was so gracious and kindly and loving to everyone that her husband had her killed because her joyful universal love had not singled the Duke out for somehow reverencing his bigger-than-life image he had fostered. Like an old lady tending her brilliant Queen Anne rose in the front of her house.

"Mrs. Wainwright, there's something...."

"Just call me Gina, Father."

"I don't understand. Doesn't your husband know—from the last time you were intimate—that he is the father of this child?"

Gina looked to the right, out towards the Jesus statue—as though she were drawing strength from the Lord Jesus it represented. Maybe there was something more here.

And there was.

She turned back to Father Wolfe with a look that would have melted the desiccate heart of Adolf Hitler. "Father, Gene is an alcoholic. But he's not your garden variety of alcoholic. You see, he is so anxious to make the step to Governor—and then maybe the White House itself—that he stays away from drink for sometimes long periods of time—which goes to show, I guess, the tremendous power of our wills. And then"—she turned and looked out at the Jesus statue again—"he goes the whole way. He loves his Jim Beam, and he drinks and drinks and drinks. Usually when there's no one else around—except me. And often enough he blacks out. What we talked about or did while he was out of it, he has no recollection of the next day—or whenever he comes back to his senses. And that's what happened, Father—that night God gave us another child. And Gene had no recollection whatsoever of our making love. And so he cannot see how the baby I am carrying is his when he knows of nothing on his part that brought it about. No, Father, believe me: I have not been unfaithful." Her eyes were brimming with tears as she looked like a searchlight into the old priest's eyes.

"But since he thinks it can't be his, he wants rid of it lest the knowledge that anyone might have that he had been cuckolded—that is the right word, isn't it Father?—would ruin his political chances."

"That's the word, all right.

"Well, you must not get an abortion."

"You're right, Father. But he is so insistent, Father."

"Will he get physical, force you?"

"Oh, I don't think so, Father. Gene has always been a gentleman and a kindly husband to me. Gentle. Thoughtful. I know he won't do anything violent with me. Besides, it's liable to get in the papers. The law says that abortion is OK. But it also says that assault, abduction, physical attacks are not.

"Father, what can I do? It will probably be his last child—I am getting almost too old to become pregnant again. And it has been so long since we had Benjy."

"Fifteen years."

"Yes. We were hoping to have more children. I wanted them. Gene said he wanted them. And God never granted them to us. And finally when we probably can't have any more, we do have that child."

Not the least bit sleepy now. So much to run through my gray matter.

Would a letter to Chollie help? I certainly am not going down to the fridge again.

TWENTY-FIVE

Chollie,

Forgot to tell you about the big bash I had been invited to.

Sorry I haven't written to you today. Is it still today or Tuesday already? But then, since you are with God—if you aren't, who is?—time is irrelevant, isn't it? That's what one of the boys today wanted me to get into.

And as you well know, I find it much more helpful to write out these prayers to you—how long has it been since you have gone to meet the good God?—than to try to just think them or even pray to you about them.

Anyway.

The affair this evening—yesterday evening—Monday evening; I'm too tired to try to straighten it out—was at the Senator's home on north Kennedy Drive–the name the city fathers had substituted for plain old Main when Kennedy was murdered. But I've reminded you of that already. Large. Palatial. New. With mostly comfortable—and expensive-looking black leather chairs and couches. Lithos on the wall. A large Van Gogh and a Matisse or two. And the chandelier for the entrance foyer that easily accommodated thirty people was huge, delicately filigreed and bright gold.

I must have gotten there about eight—and things were just about to get started.

The Senator was there at the door to welcome all of us. With a smile and a handshake and a "You're my old friend" touch to your elbow.

Yes, I was wearing my Roman collar. The Senator, even though a Democrat, has long been a pro-life champion. He had personally phoned—not just the written invitation his secretary had sent–and asked that I come to support him. As you well know, I hate big parties. Talk just to make talk seems like such a waste of time. But I could hardly pass up this golden opportunity to support his pro-life stand.

Conspicuously absent was his wife Gina.

And I was immediately taken back a year or so when the Senator had offered a fête at his home to celebrate his winning his Senate seat. And after the Senator had welcomed us as we had come in the front door, he left to go upstairs. And down that long and elegant staircase he came hand in hand with his beloved Gina. He was very much in love. And he was ever so delighted to have her as his wife. And well he might be. She was simply a lovely lady—everything a politician could want in a wife. And I do not mean that in a demeaning way: any public figure would have enjoyed her beautiful support—that was at the same time deferential and modest and quiet. For all of her pushing forty years, she still had the slim figure of a twenty-year-old Grace Kelly and all the innocence of a little girl in her grandmother face—yes, yes, she was not a grandmother, but she had that look that grandmothers get when they take up their tiny grandchildren in their arms.

But this evening she was not there, of course. And it was somehow a black hole—a brilliant star that had been and was no longer—to all that was going on.

And as I stood there, martini in one hand and a salami/Swiss cheese/olive on a toothpicked hors d'oeuvre in the other, I found myself in a small group of Kino graduates. Jim Kelly, Armando Ordañez, Julian Fritz and Shane Nguyen. I think you had Shane and Armando in your freshman theology class. And as they reminisced and kidded me about old classroom incidents, I found a strange current in the overall sea of sound.

In the group next to us was a very blonde woman of about twenty-five or so—if you can really ever tell a woman's age within ten years—who was orating—that's the best word I can find for it—to the rest of her group. She had one of those voices you could hear whispering on the other side of a soccer field—grating, sharp and penetrating. Never would she under any circumstances need a PA.

"I'd give anything to have him." She laughed—a tough male tympan. She was not very tall, but seemed as tall as any of the men in her group. She has a valentine-heart face that could break your heart but that was somehow hard and male-like—in spite of the remarkably long eyelashes—were they her own? And everyone in the group laughed. "I would claw my way through the jungle if that would do any good. I want him. I'd kill to get him." The him, it became evident when heads turned in his direction, was Senator Wainwright. Her hard eyes gleamed a little when she said that—bright eyes in a beautiful but tough face. And then she laughed–a hard, TV-wrestler laugh again just a note or two higher on the scale. And everyone in the group with her laughed a little too boisterously.

I wondered why she was there in a new guise—this woman I had met on my prior visit was a maid then. So I asked Julian Fritz (from the class of 1990 and already a lawyer to be reckoned with) why the maid was there in an evening dress. "She's the representative of the restaurant-help union—they call themselves associates—and the Senator wanted her here to see if in this guise she could net him more votes."

I found myself standing next to her when the speeches were about to begin. "Did you?" Nothing, I felt, like clearing the air with a candid question.

She backed away from me. "Did I what?"

"Kill her? To get him."

That's when I really found out that her voice would do well on a soccer field. "Who the hell do you think you are? Just because you're wearing that funny collar doesn't mean that you can ask me to make some sort of a public confession to something I obviously didn't do." Her pretty heart-shaped face straightened–and hardened even more. "Who do you think you are?" And then she lowered her voice. I never before knew the meaning of smoldering eyes. But now I know. As if her eyes were trying to bore right through me, they were sharp and hard and tightly focused on my eyes. "No, I didn't. How could I have? But"—and the tough lines of her face relaxed a little in a half-smile—"but I would have. And I could have." It seemed to be the wrong order of things. But that's what she said. And then she laughed that deep laugh again. And it seemed to somehow calm her down—like the air spilling out of a puncture in a bicycle tire.

She probably would have said more. But the Senator was up at the lectern and tapping the microphone, and when I heard the tap from the speakers was asking us to "listen up."

I had asked her that stupid question—how could I have expected a straight answer?—because as soon as she had spoken her piece to that adjacent group, I was taken back a month or two when I had been a guest at the Senator's mansion—this for a much quieter soiree. And this same woman who was now a part of the important guests—except, of course our humble servant, yours truly—was doing the serving along with another woman about her same age. Very proper maid's outfits: black dress and lacy cuffs and starched, nun-like coifs.

The other maid was unremarkable. But this woman wore a dress—albeit black—that threatened at any moment to split somewhere, so tight was it. And what was under it could hardly fail to catch any male's eye. But the interesting thing was that when I had quietly asked the Senator to use his bathroom for the usual purposes and he had directed me there, as I was coming back, I heard voices from the contiguous kitchen. It was the same soccer-field voice, but very quiet this time—scarcely loud enough for me to hear it. And she was saying, "He's mine. That's the man I want." And she laughed, and there was a murmur of another voice. But she interrupted. "None of this waiting-on-table stuff. I want everything that goes with being the wife of this state's Governor." Another bit of murmuring. Yes, I was eavesdropping and I shouldn't have been, but I was fascinated. "Of course I know he's crazy about his wife. But we'll have to get rid of her somehow, won't we?" And she laughed again. Louder.

Her voice was coming closer, and so I quietly proceeded on my way.

I was hardly back with the Senator, his wife, her mother and Benjy when she appeared with more hot coffee to go with the tiny and delicious ham sandwiches.

And then I was back to the reality of the Senator last night.

"I want to thank you all for being here tonight. And I hope that I can count on all of you to take my message to as many voters as you can.

"Before I can say anything else, I want you to know that I really miss Gina at my side as I make this announcement to you. I was crushed to learn of her death. And I considered postponing this evening. But we're almost out of time and I know that Gina would want us to go on: she dreamed of my being the Governor of Arizona." But there somehow was not even the trace of anguish in his voice. Not even the faked kind.

And I asked myself how he could be so cold and distant about the cruel death of the wife he had always doted on. What had changed him?

TWENTY-SIX

"As you know from my voting record in the Senate, I stand for justice—justice for everyone—above all in this our wonderful State of Arizona.

"And I know that you will all agree that this in a particular way applies to undocumented aliens and marginalized school children and the elderly who can no longer take care of themselves. And those of every racial origin."

And there in corner of the foyer stood Lyda Lott, all six-feet-plus of her, and her camerawoman taping all of this.

"But what you do not know is that under the guidance of my fellow Democrats across the nation, I have found it most important to change my unjust attitude toward women. Until now I denied them their freedom by—and now I am sorry to say it—being very overtly what some people call pro-life. But it certainly has not been pro-life for women's lives. And this evening I want to publicly make it clear to all of you that to give women the equality that is deservedly theirs, my voting from now on will be pro-choice. I am aligning my posture with the Supreme Court of the Yewnited States of America." (I know, I know. He was being serious. But that bit of the South—I think he's from Memphis—he still carries with himself when he talks about his country.) A quiet murmur rippled through the crowd. Pleasant? Unpleasant? It was hard to tell. Puzzled *was probably the right word.* Guidance *was a nice word–guidance of his fellow Democrats–I had to hand it to him.*

"Senator." I was angry. Outraged. I was being used: here I was a priest—officially in my blacks and white collar. How could someone be so petty as to use the Church—and its perennial teaching of Jesus Christ's love for life—to foist on others the Senator's sudden love of death? I was surprised to hear myself speaking. And I was using my "I am the authority in here" classroom voice. What was pushing inside me? And suddenly I heard inside, deep inside me, the voice of Janey Peers that urged me years and years ago to show my real love for her by going off and becoming a priest. Was it Janey? Was it the Holy Spirit? Was it my conscience?

"Pro-choice gives no choice to the murdered baby. Pro-choice is pro-murder. You're a Catholic. You know this."

Suddenly there was a lot of loud talking going on around me. But that was enough. I left. I didn't want to get into some kind of debate. Or a big hassle. And I saw that the only one who was left with me was Julian Fritz, the quiet kid who had sat by the door in 1990. We walked out together.

Luke

TWENTY-SEVEN

"Hiya, Father." Big smile. Loud voice. It was Tony Santos, of course. And he had his hand on the shoulder of the much smaller innocent-faced Mother Teresa girl. Anyone from either school could tell you that from her blue-plaid jumper and white blouse. It was Rita Poulos, of course.

After his letter to Chollie, Father Luke had slept like a man in a coma until the alarm sounded reveille right in his ear at 5:01—he hated to get up at the unbelievable hour of 5:00—on Tuesday morning. And even if that was not enough sleep, he felt much fresher than he had the day before.

"You're all over the papers and TV this morning, Father. Did you know that?"

"No. What's it all about."

"Well"—this was Rita, her bright, black eyes laughing—"bottom of the front page was a story about the priest who had broken up Senator Wainwright's campaign-opening party last night by telling the Senator that as a Catholic he should be pro-life."

Tony couldn't leave it to her alone. "And Moroney in his 'My Side' column in the *Observer*'s local news section talked about a priest who had a lot of guts to speak out but was stupidly out of tune with the American conscience and its politics."

Rita smiled her pert smile around her a-little-too-large Greek nose. "And Andy Feller in this morning's newscast said that Father Luke Wolfe, a teacher at Kino Prep had broken up Senator Wainwright's candidacy-announcement meeting by shouting that as a Catholic the senator should remain pro-life."

"Gotta see the little lady safely off to Mother Teresa, Father. Catch you later."

"Good-bye, Father." Rita smiled with her dancing eyes again.

Their smiles would leave anyone—even Jean-Paul Sartre—with the prospect of a wonderful day to come.

His cell phone warbled, and he went over to his desk to answer it. "Father." It was Captain Parsons, and Father Wolfe in imagination could easily see him stroking down his luxuriant mustache as he talked. "What gives with the Mohr—he said it MO-her—kids? Their parents are frantic. And we have searched all over. Couldn't get to your Dean Van Steen—I can understand why his phone is unlisted—last night to find out where or when they had last been seen at your place. He told me that they had had your class during first hour and had showed up for second period math—the last time either of their names had shown up as present on the absentee reports."

"Ohohoh." Father Wolfe sat down heavily at his desk. "Just before I phoned you to tell you about their bizarre information, the two of them left my classroom, even though I told them to stay. And I sent out one of the seniors to look for them as soon as I noticed they had left. I just took it for granted—stupid me!—that they did not want to talk to me—but were going to their next classes—wherever—around the school. Stupid me."

"Well, they have disappeared. Any ideas?"

"I wish. Keep me up to date. Please. I'll do what snooping I can around and amongst the kids. And let you know."

Well, at least the Captain hadn't worried about last night's confrontation with Wainwright.

He had scarcely finished with Captain Parsons when the phone demanded attention again.

It was Father Sloan, the principal. "Father, please come to my office immediately." It sounded like St. Peter's summons to the final reckoning.

It was the first period and number six on the schedule. "But, Gerry, I have class now. Sophomores"—he glanced at the clock with the birdsong at every hour, the gift of Hans Schlacter from last year—"in just a few minutes."

"Father, please come to my office immediately. My secretary will sub for you."

She was already there at the door. "I'm on my way right now, Father." And he gently pushed the "END" button.

"Good morning, Mrs. Bates."

"Father." And she smiled her always gracious all-will-soon-be-right-with-the-world-and-God smile.

"All right, guys. Study anything you want until I return. And don't give Mrs. Bates any trouble."

Down to the end of the hall, into the main office, past the desk with the quiet but elegant stand-up sign "Mrs. Amy Bates" on it, next to it a large jar of gumdrops for the ever-ravenous males who came to her for transcripts and the like, and next to that a large elegant rose in a dainty vase. Then around the end of the counter to the open door of the principal's office.

TWENTY-EIGHT

"Sit down, Luke." Father Principal was not in a happy mood. He did not sit at his desk, but at the conference desk in the annex to his office. And three chairs down to his left sat Father President, Bill Blazer, not looking at either of them but facing the table in front of him. Father Sloan's usual stoic demeanor had somehow been upstaged: he looked rattled at the same time. "Father, what the hell is going on?" Gerald was usually a little more aware of the prestige of his office. He was upset.

"Where should I start?"

"Well, you could start"—Father Sloan grasped a lens of his very large and round rimless glasses and lifted them higher on his nose—"with last night when you made some kind of public spectacle of yourself. And you might go on to tell us why the police are trying to find out what you have to do with the disappearance of the Mohr twins." This was probably not the time to correct him on their precise relationship. Or the pronunciation of their name: Father Gerald said it MOH-hair. "Aren't you aware that whatever makes or breaks you reflects on the whole school?"

Why try to answer the latter question? "Well, I was asked personally by Senator Wainwright to attend last night's campaign-opening bash at his place. Precisely because I am a teacher of his son. And he said he wanted me there because I am a teacher here: he hoped that my influence with the teachers here and all the old grads that I once had in class over the last forty years here would help to boost his votes."

Father Sloan, with his right fist on his cheek like Rodin's *Thinker*, looked thoughtfully down at his desk. Clearly, there was nothing wrong with that.

Father Blazer looked up from the desk in front of him and stared with his little-boy innocent look at Father Wolfe. But he said nothing. He was a firm believer in subsidiarity.

"And then he—the Senator—said he had changed his stance with regard to abortion. And I thought something should be said. Especially since he has always publicly insisted that he is a staunch Catholic."

"Umph. It's not always necessary to voice the Catholic position on everything or everywhere, Father." He straightened his glasses again and looked directly at Father Wolfe. "And, besides, that's Bishop Klein's job. Did he say anything?"

"He wasn't there. Maybe he was sick. Maybe he was busy with Confirmations someplace. Maybe he just didn't feel like coming. Maybe he wasn't invited. But he wasn't there.

"So I felt I had no other choice. As a Catholic. As a priest. Wearing my Roman collar. I suddenly realized I was being used. I got angry deep down. A Catholic priest there in uniform, even, to silently witness the Senator's denial of everything we Catholics hold. What would people think if they saw him mutely supporting the horror of murder on demand? Isn't that the scandal Jesus talks about? And the millstone? What else could I do but speak out?"

Jesus, why do I have to be uppity? I have no right to the stance that says I know it all.

"Father, please remember that you carry the reputation of Kino on your shoulders wherever you go—for all the world to see. And, as I said, we do not have to speak up every time someone challenges our Catholic stand."

I'm sure glad you didn't say "Catholic Faith," Ger.

"Mmm. And what about the Mohr boys?" The Senator Wainwright scrutiny was over. Father Sloan pushed his tongue up under his upper lip and over his upper teeth. A sure sign he was thinking deeply about all this.

"After the boys told me how the body of Mrs. Wainwright got into our freezer, and I said I had to call the police about this, they left before I was aware of it, and I have no idea where they have gone."

"Are you sure that's all you know, Father?" Just a touch of sarcasm. And he stared at Father Luke fixedly and sharply through the topmost section of his trifocals.

Father Wolfe straightened the few stray white hairs lying fallow across his scalp and answered this insult to his integrity by looking straight into Gerry Sloan's eyes. "Yes, that's all I know."

The President followed him out of the office. In the hall, Father Blazer did have something to say. "Luke, I know all this is difficult for you to take. And it seems that Gerry is riding too hard on you. But remember that he is the best administrator we have had here since the school began. He has a gift for hiring just the right people—teachers and staff who have made Kino a prize-winning educational institution for the whole Valley. And has revamped the curriculum so that it's airtight—from the first day of freshman year to Graduation, a logical progression of building-block classes. And he visits all of you often to insist on the integrity of each of you as a teacher. And that's why he is riding you hard: he cannot understand where you're coming from. So, be patient with him. And don't be afraid—no matter your years and years of experience—to be open to the possibilities he presents to you—no matter how foreign at first they may seem." And Father Bill offered him that rich, happy, little-boy grin he was famous for.

"OK." It was obviously difficult, but Father Luke managed a wan smile.

TWENTY-NINE

He returned to his classroom. "Thank you, Mrs. Bates. You are very kind."

The sophomores had left with the class-ending bell.

"Happy to help." She smiled her happy smile and quietly left, the snapping of her skirt attesting to her usual gait that seemed to be twice as fast as anyone else's.

And the bell to begin the next class rang.

Their prayer had been brief. Harry Rivers had simply led them in a Hail Mary and "Mother of God." But the *Amen* was as loud as usual.

"All right, guys"—it was the second period of the day, number one on the schedule—"we're going to take a look at some new proper-usage rules today, then we'll review last week's test and then we'll have our test for today. Joey, put that on my desk." It was his bored fatherly-advice voice. Avuncular. Joey Fetter sat next to the back wall in the middle of the classroom.

"What, Father?" It was innocent and simple—not a drop of cynicism. And so it deserved an answer in kind.

"Whatever it is that you are showing Al and is distracting both of you." His voice dripped boredom.

"Father, I can't."

Father Wolfe had already turned away and moved toward the board at the front of the room. He stopped in surprise. "Why not?" He turned and looked at Joey. Joey's answer had betokened some sort of self-torture. And it now showed clearly in his usually half-smiling face. He was clearly embarrassed.

Joey had a baseball in his hand. "It has the signatures of Randy Johnson and Curt Schilling on it. I got them myself and I could never part with it even for a few minutes."

Father Wolfe turned and looked directly at him. Joey was very serious. Not defiantly. But still very serious. Like a dog protecting his bone. Watchful, but not yet snarling. He sounded as though the Diamondbacks were pretty close to the Blessed Trinity.

Father Wolfe laughed right out. It was half laughter. It was half surprise. And it was half "This is great fun."

"I forgot. You are in the running to be our first-string Junior Varsity pitcher, and your role models have to come from the quondam World Championship team." He straightened his forlorn wisps of white hair. He could win, of course, but was it worth it? Why make a federal case of this?

"OK." Father Luke laughed again. "But put it away so that it doesn't distract either of you——you or Al or anyone else."

He moved to the board again.

"Father, what does *quondam* mean?" That was Chris Cringle, who seemed born to ask questions out of sync with the matter at hand.

"It means beforehand, former, at a prior—"

Suddenly the classroom door opened with a wrench that seemed to make the 1928 structure sway and totter with the force of it.

"Wolfe. Father Wolfe." It was a big voice. It was a commanding voice. It was an angry voice. It was Senator Eugene Wainwright's not-to-be-trifled-with voice.

"Well, good morning, Senator. This is class time, of course." He smiled like a mother telling Johnny he must not have any more cookies. "Would you like to join the class? We were just about to learn the difference between *less* and *fewer*. Or can we talk after class?" Father Wolfe found himself surprisingly calm. Surprisingly, because the Senator was a big man, probably six-four and weighing in at what looked to be about 250 pounds with enough of that still muscle sufficient to throw someone around. And his eyes were charged with anger.

Well, I have always prayed to be a martyr—like John Brebeuf, the Jesuit the Iroquois had scalped and cut out his heart to eat to gain his courage. But this would hardly be called martyrdom—even if it might well come in a close second.

He knew he should be weak-kneed and afraid down into his bones. But he was surprised to find himself as calm as Tempe's Town Lake on an airless day.

This whole scenario showed the Senator as anything but the true gentleman Gina had sketched him. But then, she did say he was an ever-gentleman with her. Only? Only to her?

"Listen, Father—"

"Senator, this classroom hardly seems the place, and the matter at hand—the learning process the parents of these young men have paid for—should not be interrupted by something private. I will be glad to talk to you as soon as class is over." Father Wolfe found himself using the voice of an irritated father explaining to a ten-year-old boy the respect due an elder.

Am I being too repetitious? But, then, the Senator doesn't seem to get the message.

"Like hell, you will. You sniveling little snotnosed priest"—it sounded like something out of an early nineteen hundreds dime novel—"you're going to apologize right now and in public. And I have brought a reporter and camera from Channel BLOT."

That's KNOT, Senator, KNOT.

"So the whole state can see how clearly you have repented"—he paused to chuckle at his cleverness in using such an apposite and ironic verb to a priest—"of your stupididity." Was that on purpose? Did he stutter? Had he been drinking something stronger than 7UP?

The Senator had come straight in from the door and was standing in front of Father Wolfe who was still facing the class. "Well, Senator, I'm sorry but I am not going to make any statement to you or to the world until I have finished making a statement, as I have said, about the difference between *fewer* and *less* to this group of fine young men." He paused and looked at the class. "And given them a quiz on that and the similar matter of the past week."

The Senator took another small step that brought him Altoids-laid-on-Jim Beam close to Father Wolfe. "Oh, but you will." And as he raised his hand to grab Father's shirt, the door was opened again, with only a little less energy than its previous experience.

It was Ms. Lyda Lott—all six feet nine of her. She sailed in like an 1800s Captain Horatio Hornblower square rigger, breast high like the figurehead on one of those ships, and obviously afraid of nothing. She was followed by her four-foot-three chunky camerawoman—she seemed to have no name and no need of one, and possessed no personality—who seemed like a pair of very mobile legs and had a huge camera for torso and head. She already had her light on and was filming. Like the captain's launch at the ready next to the big ship.

"Senator, we want to start." Ms. Lott's voice made it clear that she was not to be trifled with.

But the Senator with his left hand had pulled Father Wolfe to himself and cocked his right hand into a huge fist.

Has he forgotten that this was to be shown to all his constituents? Had his wife been right about the totality of his alcoholic blackouts?

And that's when Joey Fetter—like a tall palm only lightly bothered by a breeze—stood up with all of his six-foot-three, 140-pound frame, and fired his best pitch ever directly at the Senator, hitting him squarely in the right temple. Was it going 90 miles an hour for the less than forty-and-a-half feet as that evening's TV news later reported?

Senator Wainwright slowly relaxed his hold on Father Luke's shirt and politely crumpled into a heap of unsupported clothes on the floor. And the whole class sighed as one. And Kyle Sunderland who sat next to Father Wolfe's desk and had been trained to phone for help whenever a situation might arise in the classroom that Father Wolfe could not cover was already up and punching 911 into Father's cell phone.

Father Wolfe bent down to check the Senator's carotid pulse. Gene Wainwright was still alive. And there seemed little else they could do until help arrived.

"Sarah—"

She does have a name.

"—have you got all of that on tape?" Lyda, no matter the circumstances, was your perfect news reporter. Never rattled. Perfectly at home in the most startling situations.

"Any comments, Father?"

"No. Not now."

"Well, I do. (Sarah, hold the tape.)"

So she has not only a name but a face, now that she had pulled back from the eye-piece, and a pretty one at that, which is pie-pan round and somehow almost nose-less. Had she spent too much time behind the camera?

"Gentlemen." Lyda sounded as though she were the President of the United States declaring war. "The Senator was upset because last night Father Wolfe defied him as a Catholic on his new stand for abortion. Father Wolfe was right, of course. But I want you all to hear from me loud and clear: abortion is a crock." She looked boldly out at the students and seemed to be addressing them individually, every one. TV reporter experience. "Believe me, I know. I don't care what Senator Wainwright said on last night's KNOT news." Was she going to explain? Again? As she had told him and this same class just a few weeks before about the botched abortion she had to live with? Maybe now she would add with a soupçon of understatement that she had to live with her conscience ever since, and the wonder of what her child would be like and be doing and finding God's love in life as he or she grew into adulthood and choosing personal God-given values.

"Ms. TV Lady." It was Gerald Carruthers. With his Einstein—but without the mop of hair—face decorated with a huge pair of steel-rimmed glasses. "What's so wrong about removing a bit of tissue that's in a woman's way?"

Why is Gerald asking this question? He's been unsuccessfully trying for a month to get some of his fellow sophomores to form a club that would shout pro-life at abortion clinics.

The navvies were manning Lyda's cannon, stuffing them with the ball and the bag of powder. "Young man, if that 'bit of tissue' was nothing more than that, how did it suddenly at birth turn into a human being? Wasn't that what you were once?"

"Well, since it's so obvious that this tissue is the squeaky beginning of a real human being, why don't politicians turn the laws around to protect this human being the same way they protect the lives of all of us already-borns?" Gerald smiled his best supercilious smile.

Got it. This tyke is really sharp. A lot sharper than I had realized. He wants the good lady to repeat again for his classmates her devastating disgust of the whole business.

Lyda Lott looked down on them from her Olympian irenic aerie as though she were Minerva, the goddess of wisdom. But her tone of voice was an elementary schoolmarm's. Her eyes swept over the recumbent Senator and then focused on the class, again somehow managing to stare with her reporter's "on the air" look into the eyes of each individual there. "If we had fewer politicians who advocated abortions, we would have less of the horror of killing unborn children." Then she dramatically swept out of the harbor, followed by the captain's skiff.

And Gerald shyly and slyly looked as if he had swallowed the proverbial canary.

Had she been listening at the door? And the class had heard a sharp-edged example for the lesson for the day as well as another abortion put-down.

The paramedics were suddenly there. With a few efficient moves, they had the Senator on a collapsible gurney and into their van and on the way to the nearest hospital.

The door closed. Quietly. Seemingly by its own power.

Those firemen are certainly efficient!

"All right, guys. Time for this week's punctuation quiz. Al, please pass out the test from the copier trough. Tyler, the Scantrons, please."

THIRTY

The bell had hardly rung to end school. For another day. Tuesday. Father Wolfe was saying adios to his sophomores, when the maid that had served at that long-ago pleasant evening with the Senator and his wife showed up at the door of his classroom. This time in a very modest white blouse and black slacks. And a big smile.

"My name is Allie Carpenter, Father. And I've come to apologize, Father. I was boorish with you last night."

"That's all right: I probably somehow deserved it." Father Wolfe straightened the white hairs.

"I'm sorry. But I also want to talk to you about my nephew. Ben Dover. His parents showed me his third-quarter report card. And it was clear he was doing reasonably well in all his other classes. But he barely squeaked through with you. His parents are now both much too ill to come and see you. Chemotherapy for Alice. Leukemia has nailed Adolph. So they asked me to come." Allie smiled a warm but somehow distant smile.

"Is there something I can do to help the boy?"

"Well, Ms. Carpenter"—

"Just call me Allie, Father."

"Ben apparently hates to write, to put himself out there on paper. I have talked to him several times about this, emphasizing how little it matters how foolish he thinks it makes him look. The only one to read the students' papers is yours truly. I tell the boys this all the time: no one but no one reads their papers except me—unless they show it to someone else themselves."

"Well, that part of it was easy, wasn't it? Now what do we do to get him to do his writing assignments?"

"I have tried, Allie. Perhaps your encouragement. And smile. And enthusiasm for a job well done might help."

"I'll do my best, Father. I hope his next marks show the difference."

"I hope so too." Father Wolfe tried to sound enthusiastic. But his memory told him that there was little hope save through his prayers: the boy simply had this hang-up.

"And I apologize again for last night, Father. You see, I so much love Gene, but could not fulfill it so long as he had this photogenic woman at his side. I wouldn't really have been willing to kill her. That's just how I felt."

"Well, I hope you didn't go along with just your feelings—as we so often do." He smiled his grandfather-giving-sage-advice-to-Little-Sissy smile.

Allie stiffened. Had he been too preachy?

"Anyway, let's both pray for Ben—that he make the most of his opportunities here at Kino."

She said nothing. An ambiguous smile. A half-wave. And she got up and walked out and down the hall.

THIRTY-ONE

Chollie,

Joey Fetter saved the day and maybe even my life when he fired that Schilling/Johnson fastball. I guess the good God figures I'm not yet ready to give my life to defend the innocent.

And our TV roving-reporter friend, Ms. Lyda Lott, was there. And her diminutive camerawoman—Sarah is her name—caught it all. And though he said nothing, Father Sloan was not at all happy when he saw it on the news tonight, even though the rest of the padres, including Father Bill Blazer—I guess I've told you a thousand times that he is Kino's president now—chuckled over it when it came on as the opening story on the six o'clock news. They even showed lanky Joey casually walking from the back of the classroom up to the prone figure of Senator Wainwright to make sure he had retrieved his precious baseball—almost sacrificed on the altar of my safety.

And the timing was perfect: we had just called the school nurse to revive the senseless Senator, when Captain Parsons arrived with Lieutenant Higgins. Had they fielded the 911? Or were they here for something else? I never did find out.

"Oh yeah. The police." That was Chris Houser–the huge sophomore who is already going bald. "Hey, man, that big guy on the floor was just about to drop Father Wolfe. Joey got him just in time. A little high for a perfect strike. But it did the job all the same."

What's with this Gene Wainwright? His wild temper seems to ruin whatever chances he had for the fulfillment of his big ambition to be Governor.

Well, while Bill Higgins marched the Senator off to jail to answer the charge of attempted assault and battery, Oscar Parsons and I met between classes to arrive at the conclusion that nobody but nobody has the least clue where the Mohr brothers are.

And no one had been able to come up with a single clue about the murderer of Gina Wainwright.

A kind of early postscript: right after the last bell Father Pierre met me at my classroom door—and then patiently waited until the last student had left. Even Peter Oudt who wanted to know why he had not answered the fewer/less *question correctly—and seemed to understand my explanation.*

"Father"—without any attempt at a preamble—"what I say...." He suddenly became aware of Allie Carpenter standing at the doorway, obviously wanting to see me. He waved her into the classroom, walked over to a desk, carried it out into the hallway, and closed the door. He made it clear he would patiently and happily wait until she was gone.

Allie was here to get help for her nephew—Ben Dover, one of my students who is having a tough time of it with English. And she again denied—no matter her earlier comments—that she had killed Gina.

When she had left, Father Pierre came back with the desk. Again without an introduction. "This is not for any kind of repetition." He looked down into my eyes and bored right into me with his clear and friendly eyes. Then he went back to the door, looked down the hall, both ways.

"I hear that Gerry was not pleased with your reaction to Senator Wainwright's speech last night." He pushed his long nose to the right as though he wanted it out of the way—as if he were searching for something to be found there—as though he were looking for the perfect way to say whatever it was he had to say. "This is not public, you understand." He again looked both ways down the empty hall. "But from what I saw on TV last night, I heartily agree with you. It reminded me"—so many things reminded him of an anecdote from his long life—"of when my father was teaching me to drive. I grew up in Chicago." He said Shih-CAH-go. The way they sing it in their theme song.

"He wanted me to be the best driver in the world. So Sunday morning after Sunday morning when we came back from Mass and had had breakfast—remind me to tell you sometime about the delicious coffeecake my mother made (his eyes took on a faraway look)—he took me to a large empty park near our house to make sure I could and did stop and start with smooth precision. We had a Model A Ford, which"—he glanced at Father Wolfe's white strands on his head—"as you undoubtedly remember, had a manual shift. He made sure that I could parallel park neatly and without hesitation with him standing in the street for me to park around him as he stood in for a left rear fender. And then he brought me to the acid test.

"In Chicago in those days on the main arterials there were five lanes, the two center ones claimed the

streetcars, and the outside ones were parking spaces for cars. And that didn't leave any space to pass these old clanging galleons of the street. To pass one, you hadda wait till you got to another arterial and its stoplight, wait for the passengers to get off and on into that extra half-lane of safety and were either on the streetcar or on the curb. I had to gently pull up next to the front of the streetcar, and as soon as the light changed, I had to pop the clutch and floor the gas at the same time—hoping I would be fast enough to avoid both the parked cars waiting for me on the other side of the street and the front of the streetcar bent on crushing me. Well, I made it." He looked down and smiled a nostalgic smile at the floor. "And you, Luke, hit the gas and popped the clutch and swung right in front of that streetcar last night. Just as I did." And he shook my hand, looked me straight in the eyes to make sure I understood that he really meant it and pushed his nose out of true again.

"I'm not criticizing Gerry's concern for the reputation of the school. I just wanted you to know that I liked your courage." And his weathered face creaked a little into a smile. "Maybe you have to be older to appreciate what you did." Which made things—somehow—a lot better.

THIRTY-TWO

And there was the funeral.

Well, the funeral—Gina Wainwright's funeral, of course—took place this evening in lieu of a wake at St. Ignatius Church. They had it in the evening—as Father Pat Francis explained in his homily—so that all of Gina's friends could attend without being restricted by their work or other daytime duties.

Well, that in one way was a mistake. You know how big St. Ignatius is. Thirteen hundred people. But it wasn't even enough with SRO. They stood all along the aisles. They filled the choir loft. And they had to open the side and front doors so that those who couldn't get in could at least hear what was going on.

Before Mass I went up to offer my condolences to the Senator, Mrs. Goodwin, Benjy and Gina's brothers—Tim and Johnny—and her sister and her family. I was surprised and gladdened that they would show after all the rancor over the will uniquely Gina's. And the Senator seems to have no family. Yes, the Senator himself was there—perhaps out on bail—but I never did find out how he had escaped the rigors of the law. Her mother was in inconsolable tears—quietly drowning one Kleenex after another. Even Benjy was crying—and you know how seldom the adolescent male prejudice against weeping of any kind escapes into a really human expression of sorrow. But the Senator was dry-eyed and apparently someplace else.

Yes, I was one of the ten concelebrants—with Bishop Klein attending in full regalia: red cassock and white surplice and red skullcap and pectoral cross up there in the sanctuary. But not joining as a concelebrant. I'm not sure why.

Pat gave a wonderful homily—you know what a moving preacher he is—in which he reminded us of Jesus' wondrous concern for anyone and everyone—from the Bethesda paralytic who didn't seem to care if he was to be cured, to the lady who was hemorrhaging and needed only to touch Jesus' gown to find herself healed. And of course he tied that to the life Gina had lived, always worried about any and every who came to her in their need. But of course, it didn't need much tying. Everyone in the church knew of this lovely lady's lovely love for everyone. I know that's redundant. But she was lovely in every way.

The Communion line was unbelievably long—that, even though there were ten Eucharist Ministers who distributed the Body and Blood of Jesus under the form of bread alone.

And the eulogies afterwards. I think they must have gone on for hours. And only ceased when still others realized the weight this was putting on all of us there. Suffice it to say that everyone had some kindness to relate.

We left for the burial rites at 8:30. Did I tell you the Mass started at 5:00? Another half hour to get to St. Thomas cemetery, where Father Pat quietly with a sprinkling of holy water commended her and her child—who was fittingly buried with her—to our loving God. It seemed only fitting. Gina had died with her child.

Luke

THIRTY-THREE

Father Wolfe—greatly refreshed from a few extra hours of sleep and his Mass that had surprisingly brought the whole world to the throne of God in prayer and sacrifice to Him—on his way to school the next morning—was it Wednesday now? Yes, it was Wednesday—stopped at the mailroom to leave the brief note of condolence he was sending out with today's mail to Ernie di Paoli ('79) who had just lost his wife to cancer—how would he be able to cope?

Mrs. Smedana–Mrs. Samantha Smedana–was still at the switchboard after ten years of serving the school and the Jesuit community with all the phone calls. "Good morning, Father."

"Good morning, Samantha. Have a rewarding and joyous Wednesday. Please reroute all my important calls to my classroom phone."

"But you don't have a classroom phone." She looked at the mini-switchboard in front of her.

"Well, then, how about via the maintenance crew's walkie-talkies?"

"You don't have one of those either, do you?"

"No, but it could be fun trying, wouldn't it?" *O Lord, here I am being mean to this kindly lady who so faithfully works for the school.* He had never told her about the cell phone. He was afraid in her garrulousness she would demand time from his classes for trivia.

"What's going on in your classes these days, Father? I saw this awful picture on the news last night. His attack certainly is not going to help his efforts to become Governor."

"I'm sure you're right, Samantha. Although I am sure the public will cut him some sort of slack in his grief over the loss of his wife."

"Father." She leaned her large Idaho potato-like body closer to the switchboard shelf. Would her jowls quiver? "You won't believe what I heard just one week ago at my other place of switchboard employment." She was the night and weekend switchboard operator for the Family Freedom abortion mill at Seventh and Mountain. "Those who, across the nation, offered the services of these homes of succor for pregnant women, had"—according to the Arizona *Observer*—"chosen a most felicitous name for the wonderful work they were doing to fulfill the hopes of the Supreme Court."

She repeated like a mantra that she hated to work there but was forced to do it "for economic reasons."

"What was it you heard, Samantha?" Father Wolfe tried not to appear to be in a hurry to get to his first class.

"Well." She was whispering now, but in a stage whisper to be sure each syllable would be heard. "I just happened to tune in on a conversation. The new doctor there after poor Doctor Curtland was killed and Doctor Brandt was put behind bars. He was talking. And at first I didn't know who was on the other end of the line. But he was mouthing"— she looked askance to first one side of Father Wolfe and then the other—"sweet nothings. Sexy sweet nothings. Ribald. Racy. Pornographic. Priapic." Mrs. Smedana seemed to be thumbing through her randy lexicon. And where had she picked up *priapic*? "And do you know who he was talking to?"

"His wife?" Perhaps that could politely let Mrs. Smedana know that he didn't care in the least and that he was overdue to be in his classroom before class started. And that she should have said "whom" rather than "who" because it was the object of the preposition *to*. But he could find no gentle words. And he tried to mask the message that immediately came to his face.

"Well." Mrs. Smedana paused for effect. "It was not his wife. It was Gina Wainwright. The Senator's lovely wife. Can you imagine that? She wasn't responding much. And soon she hung up on him. Wasn't that awful?"

"The hanging up on him?"

"No, the vile suggestion."

"Yes indeed. Have a good Wednesday. The whole day."

But the thought, like a cold-bagel-on-an-empty-stomach breakfast, sat there on his mind—something that didn't want to settle.

THIRTY-FOUR

When Father Wolfe got to his classroom, there was no one there. Surprising. No Tony. No Norm. No "twins." Was there something wrong with Wednesdays?

"Kin I use one of your computers, Father? I just need to print out what I wrote last night. Our printer died. I've got it on this yellow disk here."

Joel Stearman was so small that Father had scarcely noticed his arrival. His bowl haircut with a part right down the middle made him look like a dandy from the 1920s—without the grease.

"Sure, Jo. What's with the tie today? It's not an assembly-dress day, is it?" *Have I forgotten something? Again?*

"Gotta give a presentation in biology class."

"On a frog's innards after you have dissected him?"

"Aw, come on, Father. It's a lot more sophisticated than that centuries-old stuff. It's The Effect of Automobile Exhaust Particles on the Retina of the Human Eye." He looked back down at the computer in front of him. "Where do you turn this on, Father?"

Father smiled. "The power strip there next to the last computer by the windows—on the left." Another student who seemed unable to grasp the most fundamental principle of the computer world.

The warning bell rang. "Just finished, Father." Joel sauntered to the printer, and picked up his talk.

"See you after Break, Father."

THIRTY-FIVE

A sign. Leprechaun-like Troy Wintergreen was holding up a sign. Written in bold letters on a piece of lined binder paper. "KEEP SILENCE TODAY—ALL DAY—TO STAND UP AND SHUT UP FOR EQUALITY FOR HOMOSEXUALS."

Class was just starting—first for the day and fifth on the schedule. The seniors had stood up to say the morning prayer. It was led by one of the students in the Dean's office and broadcast over the PA to the whole school. And Troy Wintergreen had not sat down with the rest afterwards.

"Well, Troy, it's going to be hard for you—getting all those *F*'s if you can't answer questions." *Should I have let my irritation show?*

Troy sat down and wrote furiously and presented a new sign. "THEN I SHALL GLADLY SACRIFICE MYSELF FOR THE CAUSE."

"What's going on?" Harry Smathers turned around to see which mute classmate Father Wolfe was talking to. "Aw, come on, Troy. What kind of game are you playing?

"Harry"—Phil Brandon was not to be kept out of it—"I'm not doing the silence thing—I think it is too much to ask from some of us..."

"Out to lunch. Intellectually. Morally." Harry was getting angry.

Well, let's see where this is going. Maybe I won't even have to comment. Maybe they'll argue it out all straight.

"...but Troy and the guys who are keeping quiet"—that Harry's comment was completely ignored clearly irritated him only further—"I think they have a point: we should look without bias on homosexuals in every phase of our American life." It was not hard to find the Debating Club manifesting itself in Phil.

"So you don't believe enough in their cause to go along with them to button your lips." Harry was not to be trifled with. Father Wolfe smiled.

But Phil casually and quietly again ignored Harry. "We insist that just because someone is 'different'"—with a slight pause and a raised pitch, he put quote marks around the word—"is no reason to deny him or her the basic freedom we Americans cherish. Women. Their right to the same wage a male gets, or their choice to find their freedom in abortion if they want. The handicapped. Blacks." Phil looked over at Harry and smiled.

"Whoa. And blacks? My friend, you are mixing cats and polar bears. And cacti and cottonwoods."

"Not at all."

The class was enjoying this. And Troy had a smile on his face that said he was in the catbird's seat: he didn't have to join in, and Phil would undoubtedly save the day.

"Look, man, blacks have no choice in the matter. The color of their skin is something they can do nothing about. Yes, they want to be treated the same as whites and Orientals and Native Americans. Just as a woman should have the same pay for the same amount of work. But not to an abortion—that's a child's death. A wholly new element you're adding here."

"Now, don't get excited, Harry." Phil smiled a warm but superior smile on him.

"Why shouldn't I get excited? Homosexuals cannot help their misplaced sexual orientation. But neither can alcoholics. Or kleptomaniacs. But the fulfillment of their misguided desires—the fulfillment—of their desires is just that—just for the sake of their desires—that's what's immoral. Just like robbing and raping and destroying somebody else's good name is immoral. Evil. Pure evil—now, there's an oxymoron for you—I guess I should have said 'complete and entire.'"

Well, this is interesting. Harry has clearly thought this through.

"Harry, take it easy." Phil made his condescending look very mature.

"No, I will not take it easy. You put homosexuals in the same category with blacks. But being black is a way of being. It's got nothing to do with right or wrong. Like being a man or a woman. Or Irish or Italian.

"But homosexuals have an inclination to do evil. If they live the gay life, they do that evil. They have substituted their desire for their conscience. But if a kleptomaniac does this, we put him in a funny farm. If a lust-inflamed man rapes, we put him behind bars. If an angry man murders, we put him in the slammer for all his days, or in some places they give him a particularly hot chair to enjoy. And they used to take care of this by stretching his neck rather substantially."

"Harry, all of this I understand. And any honest gay will agree that there is a difference, but—"

"Phil, I said you were mixing up cacti and cottonwoods. I did say that, didn't I, Father?"

Father Wolfe smiled. "Something like that."

"Well." Harry took a deep breath. "There's nothing morally wrong in itself with having a perverted inclination. Like wanting to steal. Being a homosexual. Wanting to get drunk. Wanting to rape. We all have them. Temptations to do wrong. To do evil things because of our appetites. What's wrong is the fulfillment."

I hope he doesn't run down. Ever.

"And the real problem comes when we examine where these people are coming from. If they think that robbery or pigging out is fun and games, well, we here in the land of the free say they have a right to their opinion. And just because they have that opinion or that inclination, they should not have prejudicial judgments lowered on them in their work place or their neighborhood."

"Harry, this is not the problem. The problem is that some people are saying these people with this inclination—it has nothing to do with the fulfilling of their desires—should not be hired as teachers. Or Boy Scout leaders. Or just hired."

"Just the inclination? No problem. But would you want a man who was openly and expressly insisting that the moral law is a figment of our imagination to be teaching your kids? That murder is a good idea—even if I don't do it. Or grand larceny is just like paintball wars—even if you do neither? Do you want such people teaching your kids to grow up into honest citizens? Or what do you think about your kids playing in the front yard now that a guy convicted of child abuse is living in the neighborhood?

"Do I make the irony clear, Father?"

"Looks that way, Harry."

"Harry, you don't seem to understand."

"I do. My father is a plumber. He runs a plumbing company: Smathers Pipes—no apostrophe after Smathers because it isn't possessive: he is the company. Right, Father?"

Harry looked at Father, but never paused for his reply.

"And whenever the subject of homosexuals leading a gay lifestyle comes up, he smiles a little. 'Well,' he says, 'Our sexual powers are designed to bring life. So never hire anyone living a gay lifestyle as a plumber. He has no notion of how the plumbing is supposed to work!'"

There was a slight pause as though the class could not believe what they had heard. And then they exploded in laughter.

And the bell rang.

Well, that certainly was interesting. Harry's eloquence sidetracked his leading the class in the understanding of his assignment—"Gunga Din"—but it was undoubtedly worth it—as well as the next couple of pages of Othello *we might have gotten through. I hope Troy and Phil got the point. They should have: it wasn't one of their teachers from the impregnable castle of academe looking down on these poor mortals. But it was one of their fellow students. And one who knew in a very concrete way the travesty and stupidity of prejudice.*

Father felt no need to add to what Harry had said, so eloquent was his posture and logic. And as an Afro-American in America, he could cover his bet like no one else except another black.

THIRTY-SIX

Funny how the memory worked. He hadn't thought about the incident for years. And then Harry's comments had brought it sharply back to him. He must have been all of ten years old. And his father had collected a scattershot array of tools—hand tools—in his workshop on the back inside wall of their garage in San Francisco.

The tools his father had cadged from one place or another. It was, after all, Depression time, and money for new tools was hard to come by. One day he had suddenly stopped the car in the middle of a street—nobody was around—and picked up a very nice screwdriver that someone had lost. So he appreciated each of his "expensive" tools. Like the hammer with its old hand-carved handle his father-in-law had given him.

And he wanted his son Luke to be able to use these tools—he often asked the boy to help build this or that, to repair one thing or another, to add something onto the house or the garage.

And then one day his father came into his workshop where Luke had been working on taking a screw out of something or other. And suddenly Luke realized that his usually quiet and calm father was very angry. What was he doing using a wood chisel for a screwdriver? And of course by that time the honed working edge of the chisel was a ragged series of dents where the slick cutting edge should have been. Luke learned the lesson of his usually peaceful father: use the tools, yes, but what they were designed for.

It was his first remembered lesson in "the end justifies the means." Not just the mediate end. But the ultimate end. The chisel was ultimately designed to gracefully—often with the help of a hammer—sculpt what you were working on—wood or some material soft enough to be cut—and often turn the debris into long, curling strips. And it didn't matter if Luke's use of the chisel was perhaps attaining his immediate goal: it was denying the ultimate goal.

Like the 400-pound man who found great pleasure in intussuscepting a fat-filled hamburger and denied the purpose of food: preservation of life.

So with homosexuality. Sure, pleasure was the goal. But as Harry pointed out from his quote from his plumber father, to say that pleasure was the ultimate goal of our sexual poseurs was to deny the deeper ultimate goal of properly using the power to bring about life.

Like the abortion that achieved the immediate goal of freedom and denied the further and real goal of sanctifying life wherever it was to be found.

Was this what made Jesuits often seem so different to others? This fixation on the ultimate end—the Greater Glory of God before all else. The end that justified giving of one's whole life to try to obtain it.

THIRTY-SEVEN

Father Wolfe had just come back from Break with a cup of coffee. He put it on his desk and plugged his cellphone into the charger. A moment later it chirped.

"Father, this is the—um—triplets."

"Where are you?"

"Safe and sound, Father. But we wanted you..."

"...to know something." How were they doing their double-voice thing? Did they have access to a telephone they could program for a conference? Or were they simply holding the phone between them? Probably some sophisticated electronic device these two had rigged up.

The voice paused while from behind the voice came the repeated blaat and siren of a passing fire truck.

"You know, your parents are worried sick. And the police have an all-points-bulletin search out for you. Come back."

"We can't. Just yet. Tell..."

"...Mom and Dad that we still love them. We're healthy. And..."

"...we'll come back just as soon as we can."

"But what we want you to hear is most important for you to hear, Father."

"Right now we can't tell you how we..."

"...know this. But a guy just robbed the L & D bank that's..."

"...just that block and a half to the north of Kino on..."

"...Dromedary. He's on foot—don't know why he didn't take off in a car—but he's headed for Kino."

"We were gonna phone the Dean to call a lockdown. But we..."

"...were afraid he would be able to get the police..."

"...to trace the call to us. But you can call him, Father."

"And be careful."

First period—which today came right after Break—sophomores—were funneling in, putting their backpacks on the floor next to their desk and telling the latest to their buddies next to them.

"Are you sure? How did you find this out?" Yesterday's threat had been enough of that sort of thing to last a lifetime.

"Father, this is for real. Call the Dean, like, right away. And..."

"...be careful."

The PA rang the bell

"Charlie, run down to the Dean's office and tell him I hear there's an armed bank robber loose in the neighborhood. Tell him I couldn't phone him because my phone is in use. He'll probably want a lockdown."

And Charlie ran—as if he were going to break the record for the 100-yard dash.

"All right, guys, please rise for the prayer."

And all thirty-five of the sophomores did just that.

"Oh Lord, help us not to fear the person who can kill only the body, but to fear the person who can send both body and soul to hell. St. Ignatius Loyola, pray for us."

Well, that's a prayer apposite to the threat warned by the Mohr "twins."

The class unanimously shouted. "Amen." Due and proper, if perhaps not quite liturgical.

"Very good, Connor. Is Joel absent today?"

"Yes, Father. He emailed me last night to ask me to take his place." Connor's brown puppy-dog eyes were the antithesis of his prognathous chin that somehow led him into involvement in everything. And Joel obviously knew how much Connor loved to lead the class in their daily before-class prayer.

"Looks as though you are adroitly getting into Scripture. Thank you."

"Father, may I go to the bathroom?" It was John Braden, the reticent student with the uncontrollable blond hair who reluctantly, it seemed, always had the right answer whenever he was called on and was now viewing Father Wolfe apologetically from behind his glasses that were somehow too large for his thin face.

"Sure, John. But you just came in."

"I know, Father. But I got talking to the guys. Then the bell rang. And I hadda get here before you recorded me tardy. I hate to sit around after school writing those inane essays when the Dean decides to penalize you for being tardy. Or something."

"Go."

Father Wolfe picked up the cell phone again.

"We're sure. But we can't..."

"...tell you how we know. We can't do anything to protect you."

"Or we would..."

"...have. Don't let him hurt anybody, Father." And there was the click as the line went dead.

Father Wolfe pushed the school numbers and then the Dean's extension.

Best to make sure he got the message. And see what he wants to do about it.

Busy. He left a voicemail message explaining the dangerous situation.

Then he tried again, this time punching in the Dean's secretary's number.

Busy. Another message.

But this didn't admit of delay. So he started to call the principal's secretary when the PA boomed on. "Will Ignatius Loyola please come to the Dean's office immediately!" It wasn't a question. Everyone in the school knew that this was the disguised signal for a lockdown—using the name of the man who founded the Jesuits almost five hundred years ago would be meaningless to anyone outside the Jesuit school. There was someone or something threatening the lives of everyone on campus. Students and faculty had done this many times in practice and occasionally when some real danger had threatened the whole school.

Charlie was back. Breathless. "It took a while, Father. He didn't realize I was there to alert him to an emergency."

"Good going, Charlie."

No point in calling anyone now—they had been alerted by Charlie, or the police, perhaps. And there was no point in tying up more phone lines.

Father Luke immediately went to the classroom door, opened it, turned the key in the lock on the outside side of the door and then sharply pulled the door shut to make sure it latched.

"Gerry, close the window shades. Get under your desks, guys."

And suddenly Father Wolfe realized that John—John Braden—was someplace between here and the bathroom at the other end of the hall. What had he been thinking of when he had let him go? And what should he do when he returned? If he opened the door to John, he might be a hostage forced to ask to come in.

"Father Wolfe, let me in. It's me, John."

Just what he had feared. Should he tell him to fend for himself—and make certain that the rest of the class was safe? And have to wrestle with his conscience before God for the rest of his days, knowing he had been responsible perhaps for the death of one of his students? Or should he let him in with...?

"Father, let me in." The voice sounded as though its speaker was in agony.

"Skye"—he was near the door—"open the door and let John in and close it immediately. Quickly."

As soon as chubby Skyler Bleu carefully opened the door a crack, it was suddenly forced all the way open, John was pushed in, and he was followed by a short, bulky male wearing a ski mask and carrying one of those revolvers that rival the meanness of a Clint Eastwood special. Big. Long.

THIRTY-EIGHT

"Too bad for all you guys." He spun the cylinder. His left arm jumped off the gun and threw itself obliquely at the ceiling.

How does he expect to kill all of us with a six-shooter?

He moved two yards into the classroom and aimed the gun at Father Wolfe's chest. "Luke Wolfe! Well, this is my day. You don't remember me. And I'm not even going to give you my name. But if anybody goes, you go first, good Father. I had completely forgotten that you owned"—he laughed a little bark at his own wit—"this classroom." His head jerked violently to the right and with difficulty—his neck muscles strained—he pulled it back where it belonged.

"So it looks as though my revenge is going to be sweet. If the cops find me here, I'll tell them to give me wheels and a free ride from here. If they don't like that, I will have wasted the good Father before they can have me." His body did an—it was clearly involuntary—Elvis Presley hip twist. "And all the rest of you guys. No point in leaving any witnesses. Stand up, all of you. We don't want any witnesses, now do we?" It was hardly a question. "I know, I know, a six-gun can't kill more than six of you. Maybe. But it would sure be fun trying. Wouldn't it?"

His head snapped to face the ceiling, his eyes bugged for a moment, his mouth stretched in a huge yawn.

This guy has to be on drugs. Or the wires are down to his head. Or something. Lord, take care of all of us.

The class hesitatingly scrambled out from under their desks.

"Whoever you are, don't do this. Give me your—" Why wasn't he feeling fear? The same cool reaction as yesterday. And here he was faced with certain death.

"Much closer, Father. Much closer. I don't want to take the least chance of missing."

"Who are you?"

"Without this mask you'd recognize me right away. And remember how mean you said I could be? You gave me an *F* for both semesters, Father. Because I refused to read your childish books and write those silly essays. And always in letter form to some fictitious person. 'Prove that Hamlet was really insane or only shammed it.' 'When did Macbeth irrevocably commit himself to evil?' See, I even remember all of those travesties." The hand with the gun in it shook uncontrollably. "Nice word—*travesties*—hunh?

"And you publicly averred—that was one of your childish vocabulary words, wasn't it?—so my buddies later told me, that it was a mean thing to flatten that little freshman who had slipped in front of me in the line at the Snackeree—or do they still call the local Sloppy Joe's by that pedantic pseudonym? Nice alliteration, hunh? See, I do remember some of those things you tried to teach us." A low chuckle filtered through the mask. "Mean? Why should he get his hamburger before me?" He reached out with his left hand, apparently to scratch his ear, but his hand got the wrong ticket and he missed by a foot and half to the left of the ear.

There was a slight movement and a cough to the masked man's left. He turned slightly that way. And with that advantage, Joey Fetter repeated the prior day's performance. As soon as the intruder became aware of Joey's movement, it was too late. He turned towards him and got the blitzed ball straight between the eyes and quietly folded to the floor. With the same singular lack of dignity exhibited the day before by the Senator.

Kyle Sunderland was already across the classroom and punching into the cell phone the disaster number. Skyler Bleu was tying up the intruder's hands with Joel Stearman's tie—Joel should have an easy time of explaining his lack of proper attire to Mr. Semlic, the biology teacher. And then there was a key in the lock, and Captain Parsons, Glock drawn, was followed by Lieutenant Higgins and the Dean and of course Lyda Lott and her camerawoman, Sarah.

Captain Parsons checked the Boy Scout square knot on the hands and pulled off the intruder's mask. He turned the comatose body over enough to see his face. Already both of his eyes were swelling. The Captain grunted a half laugh. "Know him, Father?"

"I don't think so. He says I had him in class, and he knew the sort of thing I have the students write about. But sometimes it's hard to remember faces. To judge from his age, if he did go to Kino, he would have been about Lieutenant Higgins' time. Check with him."

The Mohr brothers had been right. How did they know?

"Can't remember that I have ever seen him before." Lieutenant Higgins squinched his eyes in his attempt at memory. "Nope."

Parsons and Higgins had the intruder on his unwilling feet.

"You know the Father?" Parsons was angry. "He says he does not recognize you."

"Hah." It sounded like what you'd expect in Emperor Nero's voice. And that was all they got out of him then.

And they were suddenly gone. Father Wolfe relaxed. "I think we should grant Joey Fetter the William Tell Award."

"You mean the guy with the bow and arrow and the apple on his son's head?" That was Clark Clarke talking. "Or how about, like, the David Prize—you know, the guy who did the job on Goliath?"

"Right on, Clark." Father Wolfe smiled. It was easy to get his name right.

And the class fell exhaustedly back into their desk chairs.

THIRTY-NINE

"Father." It was Larry Curtland. The bell after the last class of the day had hardly rung. Father Wolfe sat down heavily in his desk chair and reminded himself that he had to stay behind after school in the classroom to get a little caught up on paper correcting and what was going to happen in class tomorrow—was it Thursday? He checked the school calendar on the wall beside his desk. Yes, it was Thursday.

"Larry." Father Wolfe smiled. It was easy to do that now that Larry was back to his old self. The pre-emptive attempt on his father's life seemed more and more like a bad dream. He had felt justified in trying to shoot his abortionist father and all abortionists—until Rita Poulos had graphically shown him the forgiving Christ.

"I—uh—kin I sit down?"

"Sure. Grab any desk." And Father Luke got up from his teacher's desk and sat in a student desk he had turned to face Larry.

"Two things I wanna ask you."

"Fire away."

"Well, the first is that I've been thinking about Greg Farrell's decision. To live someplace where he won't receive the benefits—financial—of his father's abortion money. And so I have been thinking about the same thing. Should I leave Mom and live with Grandma Marie or Aunt Sophie—who I think—both—would be glad to have me? And I could get a job to help offset the cost of boarding me, although I'm not sure where I will get the tuition money. I know the school somehow matches and so doubles the money a student makes outside of school if he puts his paycheck into Kino's hands."

"Sounds like a good idea, Lar. But it's your choice to make. After all, Mom will be alone now, and you don't want her to feel abandoned. And besides, there's no way you can give the money your father made in this messy business back to his—um— clients. Are you ready to give up your Beemer Z3? Let me know what you decide. Or what I can do to help you."

Am I being too impersonal? Should we spend more time on these pros and cons? And yet I do feel he must make this decision himself.

"Why don't you put this before the Lord when you go to Mass in the mornings?"

"OK." Larry's eyes turned aside from the priest's face and seemed to go on a tour to some distant place like OZ.

"Let the Lord struggle with it so you don't have to."

He was again looking at Father Wolfe. "OK."

"And there's this other thing."

"After going to Mass for a bit, you have begun to wonder if you should be a priest."

"Right on, Father." He looked up from under his brush of red hair. "How did you know?" His thin mouth turned up in a smile of surprise.

"Well, I didn't, Lar. But I wondered. What has brought you to this?"

"I dunno, Father. But I have been considering. You see, I have fallen in love with Rita. But it's something different from what the guys talk about when they talk about 'falling in love.' I don't particularly want to go out on dates with her. Or dancing. But I reverence her like an angel. She is so good. And holy. And a real human being. When I have danced with her a couple of times, I am almost afraid to touch her. You know, the way you are with a shrine. Or the picture of a Saint. Or meeting a real Saint. You know what I mean, Father?"

"Yes." And Father Wolfe segued back to his high school days again when the Janey Peers he was so crazy about knew he should enter the seminary. Yes, he had really flipped over her. But present had been the same kind of awe and reticence. Janey Peers had made it clear she was deeply in love with Luke Wolfe. And yet she was so much in love with Luke that she had intuited that God was calling him to something out and beyond their boy-girl fulfillment. And as much as he loved to take her dancing and ice skating and watching a movie, he had felt much the same way about her as Larry said he felt about Rita: she was almost too holy to touch.

"And I wonder if God is saying something to me through this different kind of love.

"Besides, there's my father." He fastened those bright green eyes on Father Wolfe's. "I don't know of any other way of really making it up to my father and to God my Father that I wanted to kill him. The man who with all his failures brought me to be.

"And the un-fun attached to that poverty, chastity and obedience thing would be a great way to try to make up for the horrible things my father was doing. Isn't that what St. Paul said: my pain making up what is lacking to the suffering of Christ?"

"Well, Larry, I think you would make a terrific priest. "Certainly better than I am. I had no such deep spiritual motivation when I went off to the seminary.

"But you would make a wonderful father and husband too. Why don't you continue to leave this in God's hands at Mass, Lar, and ask God to show you the way He wants you to serve Him? We can talk about this whenever you'd like.

"But don't let Tony know. I wouldn't be surprised if he's jealous of you—the way you look at Rita."

"You're kidding."

"No. You really do betray a kind of absent-minded adoration when you look at her."

"I thought nobody knew. You don't suppose Tony is really jealous, do you?"

"Ask him."

"Umm."

"And I will lean on the good Lord to show you where to find Him completely in your life."

FORTY

"Well, this is luck. The lady at the switchboard told me you didn't answer your room telephone—your room phone here in the Jesuit house—and you don't have a classroom phone yet. I guess you were on the way over here." He was coming down the stairs from the switchboard.

Father Wolfe was coming up the front steps of the Jesuit house, both arms full of papers and books.

"I came over to see how you were. And to just chat a little. And to see if you can help me. I need a little counseling."

"Your face is very familiar, but I just can't conjure up your name." Father Wolfe was immensely tired. He was no longer up to this morning's kind of excitement. Had he been? Ever?

"Jerry Harris." And he started to reach out his hand to shake hands only to realize that Father Wolfe was too laden to return it. "Graduated nine—no, ten—years ago. Kino's Finest, we called ourselves. Remember?"

Father Luke made the effort, but couldn't remember that use of the title. But Jerry Harris, how could he forget the tiny tyke? Like the Mohr "twins," he had looked more like a fourth grader than a high school sophomore—who always wore the happiest smile ever, even when he hadn't the foggiest idea of what the answer was that Father Wolfe had been trying to draw out of him. And he had sat on the right wing of the classroom, near the last window.

And he had returned—been assigned—to Father Wolfe's senior class two years later—and had sat in the same place. And he had grown a bit but hadn't looked much older.

But he was no longer tiny. At least six foot three, he didn't tower over Father Wolfe, but Father had to look up to him. But he was still smiling and had matured into a strikingly handsome male. Those bright brown eyes were set wide apart in a polished-apple-bright face that said "I am your friend."

"Now I've got you in the right memory space. How've you been? Keeping out of trouble?"

"Well, not trouble exactly, Father, but that's what I came to talk to you about."

"Want to sit"—Father Wolfe was very ready to sit down, anywhere—"down on one of those benches next to the Jesus statue? Or in the parlor? Or back in my classroom perhaps?"

"I want to talk to you about getting one of those annulment things."

They had settled in front of the Jesus statue. And Father Wolfe had put his armload on the bench beside him, looked down at them and with a schoolmarm's admonitory finger warned them to sit still. Jerry laughed as his mind trolled back to the English classroom in which Father Wolfe had often played that game.

"Well, Jerry, that's hardly my forte." Father Wolfe collapsed a little inside at "annulment," the word that said "failure" to the forever "I do" of marriage.

Jerry laughed. "Well, I'm glad you pronounced it correctly." Father Wolfe smiled. "How often did you correct us in class when someone said 'for-TAY'?

I unnastan"—well, although Jerry had remembered *forte*, he had forgotten how often Luke had urged them to say "under-STAND"—"but I figgered"—Father Wolfe settled into letting Jerry speak however he wanted, with no mental comment—"you could help me out of the dilemma I find myself in."

"If I can. Gladly."

"After I graduated from Kino, I went to SUA—our handy State University of Arizona. In my junior year–in the middle of November—I fell head over heels—to make use of the cliché, which right here is very fitting—with this stunningly—here's another cliché—beautiful girl. And ever so good. And ever so Catholic."

Father Wolfe smiled. Somehow they were all stunningly beautiful. Even if often they were not Catholic. And not always ever so good.

"Well, we got married two weeks after we both graduated—we were in the same class. And then she helped me get through graduate school. Me, I got a law degree while she right away went to work as a teacher. In the next four years we had three wonderful kids: Jeremiah Junior—he's still a couple of years away from Kino." Jerry smiled his dimpled trademark smile. "And Becky and Susan, cutest-ever replicas of their mother. And then about five-six months ago when the fourth one was coming along, I was delighted, but Rebecca—I never did tell you that was the name of my stunning wife, did I?—said no way. She had had more than enough of diapers. And she was having trouble enough teaching second grade over at Jefferson Elementary—she refused to stop teaching when the children came along and leaving off and picking up the kids from school and pre-school—and had no more time for wiping bottoms and cleaning Gerber's finest off the wall. So she wanted an abortion. Even though there was no need for her to go on teaching: by then I was making more than enough money to support all of us."

Jerry was staring hard at the seat beside him. "And I told her absolutely not. Well, we argued for about a week—maybe even less. And the next thing I knew was that she had packed up a couple of suitcases of clothes, thrown them into her Chevy and moved out.

"At first, I didn't know where. And then one day a week later, she called to tell me gleefully—that's the only word for it, Father—told me that just the day before she had gotten that abortion at that Family Freedom place over on Seventh and Mountain and had moved in with some guy she had met a couple of months back.

"Had those horns the cuckolded man cannot see been growing out of my head? Like in 'The Miller's Tale' in *The Canterbury Tales* we took in your class? Or had she simply found in someone else what she didn't find in me?"

Father Wolfe simply let Jerry talk and watched his face. It was no longer the adolescent unfeatured face. Now it was long and already pulled down a little on the jowls as he again stared at the bench beside him—as though the cement would frame his words for him.

"But, whatever, Father, I had been rejected. And I still love her to distraction. Literally. She often often often steps right into my mind and blows everything else away. Oh God, how I love her! Still." It was a prayer. The tears were coming now. "But what's worse is that I cannot keep my job at Beckmann and Collier. No, it's not Dewey, Cheattum and Howe."

Father Wolfe smiled in memory of the old lawyer joke.

"And take care of the kids. And I am not in love with someone else. I don't see how I ever could be." He was drawing meaningless designs—almost like a bored student scrawling in his binder, but he wasn't bored now—with his finger on the white bench.

"The obvious solution is day care. But that's no way to raise your kids. They need a woman—a warm and loving woman who really loves them to distraction, no matter the diapers and the flung food.

"And so I am in an incredible bind. And if I somehow got the Church to say that there never really was a marriage in the first place and freed me from what I had thought was a marriage true and forever, I'd hafta start looking for a new wife to take care of the kids. Like your favorite Thomas More who married another woman after his beloved first wife died and left him four children." He smiled a wintry smile and looked Father Wolfe full in the face.

"But, Father, she hasn't died. And I can't believe she did not mean that *I do* with all her heart. And the last thing I could do is swear I did not know what I was getting into or that I didn't really mean it. *I do* is *I do.* And what others might say or mean by them, that

I do was the total and irrevocable gift of myself to her. Just what old Father Atkins said in his homily at our wedding Mass."

Father Wolfe wondered if Jerry would be able to continue. His breath had become stertorous. Now the tears came slaloming down his cheeks. And he made no effort to stop them. Or clean them from his face.

"Months ago, I met this wonderful woman at her home, Senator Wainwright's palace."

Ohoh, here it comes. Jesus, take care of this poor guy.

"He—the Senator—had invited a bunch of us legal beagles to his home for supper—and undoubtedly the hope of our vote. His wife and I got talking about my problem. And she urged me to come and see you. Apparently you had stiffened her in some resolve or other to do what was right. And I wondered why I hadn't thought of that myself in the first place. She even stood there with my hands in hers and looked into my eyes and told me she would pray for me—she certainly is a motherly woman—and that everything would come out all right. And I suddenly felt as though a huge weight had been taken off my back.

"But I was hesitant to come and see you, Father. Too embarrassed, I guess.

"And then I saw her again in LA just a week or so after I had met her here—at a convention where she was giving a speech. And she again urged me to come and see you. And"—he did a careless throw-away gesture with his right hand—"here I am. Although it still took a lot of effort—and time—for me to overcome my embarrassment and come."

"I'm glad you came, Jer."

"I see no hope on the horizon. But she was right: if you can teach kids the difference between a noun and a verb, any other problems must be kid stuff for you." And he smiled that half-hearted smile again. "Kid stuff. How's that for irony? Is it a pun too?"

Father Wolfe quietly chuckled a small chuckle. He suddenly saw those ten or twelve years back when he had called on little Jerry Harris to take a sentence apart. And when he—Father Wolfe—had asked him what part of speech *desk* was, Jerry had happily responded, "A verb?" And Father Wolfe had looked out at the lawn and the Jesus statue. "Oh look, that pigeon is desking all over the Dean's car." The class had laughed with Jerry.

But right now this was something out there a little beyond a noun and a verb. And he had no simple solution. In fact, no solution at all. To try to take care of his children and work to put bread and at least a little butter on their table seemed impossible. And to swear to what was patently not true—how could you do that? He certainly meant the *I do*.

"Are there any grandmothers? Your mother? Hers? They wouldn't be a new mother. But they could make a good stand-in."

"They both live in Illinois, Father. And they are too much a part of their families in Chicago and Rockport to move here. And I could hardly move the kids back there."

"Jerry, why don't you give me a couple of days to think about this. Maybe see if I can come up with a local grandmother that might be willing to help you. Give me your phone number and email address. I see no clear path for you right now. But I will pray and trust that the Lord will enable us to find a way out of this Catch-22 situation."

FORTY-ONE

Father Luke logged off the computer. Tomorrow's quiz had needed editing.

It was 5:20, late afternoon, almost time for community Mass.

The phone rang.

"Hey, Father. Barry. *Ciao* and all that."

"Where are you?"

"Won't catch us as easily as that, Father. We have some good news. We know who the murderer of Gina Wainwright is."

"This is Terry, Father." Luke visualized him scratching his left ear. "We wanna meet with you. On one condition."

"And that is?"

"That you will tell no one about meeting us or where. And everything we tell you goes no farther than you."

"But where are you?" His voice went into the Dean of Students' mode. Distant. Cool. Calculating. "I told you before: your parents are frantic. And the police really want to talk to you."

"Terry, again. No way. *Nada. Zilch. Nichts.*" Well, those weren't quite the right words for *no*, but Father Luke understood.

"OK."

"Swear?"

"No. You'll just have take my word. You know what Jesus says about swearing."

Two voices were muttering over the phone, and, behind them, the sound of traffic with a straight-pipes

Harley that made its presence known by the exhausts' lion growl as he went past. They were obviously close to a major arterial. And Father Wolfe experienced a strange—but familiar—awareness that he could not place. Where had he experienced it before?

"OK, Father. We'll take your word. Not before, but at midnight precisely there will be a message in your mailbox in the Jesuit house telling you where to meet us. Not before. OK?"

"But how will you get into our house? By midnight it will be all locked up." For a moment Father Wolfe had forgotten the intrusion of the freezer corpse.

"Leave that to us, Father. A deal?"

"All right." He probably should have refused, but he saw no other solution to getting these kids back.

And the line went dead.

FORTY-TWO

Mass with the community that evening was a distracted one for Father Wolfe. "And, Lord, take good care of Luke and his students." It was Joe Garcia at the Prayer of the Faithful at the community Mass.

"Lord, hear our prayer."

Just as well. Luke was happy to relax a little after the full day. Even though nonagenarian Pierre Atkins was saying it: he was so alive with the simple love of Christ that it made even the weakest of his homilies fascinating and moving. This evening in his usual efficient way, he had outlined the Gospel message of the sending of the Apostles to go out and preach repentance. And he very efficiently reminded the community of our God-given vocation to do just that. "That's what our classrooms are for. To tell them all about the love of Jesus Christ."

In his quiet way he was so enthusiastic it was impossible to relax.

He said nothing about shaking their gowns free of the dust of those who would not listen.

Where were Terry and Barry? How will they get in? What did they have to tell him that was so hush-hush? *Jesus, take care of these two crazy kids, and straighten out all of this hideous business so that no one else is hurt.* He was unable to voice it at the Prayer of the Faithful. But he could and did tell that to God-become-one-of-us anyway. In silence. God understood.

Certainly.

And joining the rest of the community to share the Body and Blood of Jesus made him clearly aware that Jesus Himself was running this whole show—wherever it was going.

FORTY-THREE

After Mass they all trooped down to the TV room.

"Good evening. This is Caryntha Foley with Channel Two's Six O'clock News. KNOT.

"Tonight we will tell you about the astonishing number of wins garnered by our Diamondbacks baseball team. And we will cover that terrible gas truck accident at Dromedary and I-18. But right after this commercial, we will feature today's top story: a Kino student catches a bank robber. Will the Diamondbacks be signing up a sixteen-year-old next year? A Kino student who pitched two single hitters. Stay tuned." Her smile, so beautiful it almost seemed impossible for God to create something so lovely, was as free and open as a nine-foot-high link-wire barbed-wire-topped fence.

And they were treated to sixty seconds of cars to buy, wax to polish with, puppy biscuit and the best mouth wash in the country.

"At 10:15 this morning, Kino sophomore Joey Fetter dropped alleged bank robber Harold Gribbs. And here is Lyda Lott with the story."

The screen split. On the right screen, Lyda was facing the camera. "Kino's Joey Fetter saved the day for his teacher Father Luke Wolfe and his class of thirty-one sophomores from the threat of an armed man accused of having robbed the L & D bank at Dromedary and First Street.

"The school was in a lockdown after the police report that the suspect was at large in the neighborhood.

Once into the classroom"—Lyda could be merciful. She had not mentioned Luke's difficult decision: whether or not to let John Braden into the locked-down classroom—"when he threatened to shoot the priest and the students, Joey fired a baseball into the intruder's head that stunned him and knocked him cold long enough for the students to tie him up and for the police to arrive and escort him to jail. Joey, show our audience the weapon."

And there was Joey smiling his shy smile with the little boy dimples and holding in front of the camera the Schilling/Johnson treasure.

"Yes, this is the same boy who was featured on yesterday's news for having thwarted Senator Wainwright's attempt to get a statement out of Father Wolfe. And he stopped him in the same way. Good going, Joey." And Lyda smiled her wintry smile a little more amiably than usual. Luke was grateful that Sarah had not given them any footage of himself.

And they were back with the toothpaste and pet food.

FORTY-FOUR

"Well, Father Brown, how do you manage to get caught up in the news and leave us poor earthlings in the dust?" Father Louis Brown, the Rector, was absent this evening. No possibility of confusion. Luke looked up from his chicken soup, reached for a cracker in the center of the table and smiled at Pat. Father Pat Gallese was a radical Chesterton buff, and he saw a large measure of reality through that great thinker's ironic eyes.

"You've got the wrong guy, Pat." It was Al Friedl definitely mended from the summer's by-pass surgery: his sardonic humor was back and running. "It's just that they've got the first name confused. Luke here is in his second time around as Rex Stout's Nero Wolfe." He smiled at Joe and turned back to his soup.

Walt Whiffle couldn't keep out of it. "He just thinks he's Dorothy Sayer's Lord Peter Wimsey. Do you drive around in that 'Myrtle' car of his?"

Bill Blazer could not refrain from joining in the fun. He looked up from his salad, smiled his sad smile. "Naw, he just thinks he's that famous detective Celery Clean."

A few chuckles responded.

Luke said nothing. What could he say to this happy and personal banter?

FORTY-FIVE

Chollie,

Figured I had better start this early. Barry and Terry want to see me tonight.

Don't know if I told Jerry Harris the right thing. He stopped to see me this afternoon. Graduated about ten years ago. What a bind! He wants to do what's right, and someone else has put him in a jam he finds it impossible to extricate himself from. His wife walked out on him, and he cannot stomach the possibility of an annulment, since he once and for all had said his I do. *And now he needs someone to take care of his three kids while he is lawing it downtown at Beckmann and Collier.*

Were there grandmothers around who could take care of the kids from beginning to end of work day—keep it in the family? They both lived in Illinois. Aunts? Only Rebecca's sister—Rebecca is his wife. And ever since her nephew earned a final D in my class three years ago, she thinks I am the Saddam Hussein of Phoenix—she had told Jerry that just after she had seen me on the news after the solution to Doctor Curtland's murder.

Good friends? None close enough.

I was delighted with his insistence that he maintain his integrity before God. But what was the solution?

Well, I told him, I will look around to see if I can find a warm grandmotherly type who would just love to cherish little children again. And he must do the same.

And forget the annulment. And forget the idea of another marriage that would just confuse everything all the more. In himself. With God. And even—if you stopped to think about it—with Rebecca. Some type of mulligan?

Meanwhile, I told him to put the tykes in the best day-care he can find. And pray. And I will pray.

So, Chollie, make sure the Lord Jesus figures out a way to take care of Jerry and his tots. He wants to do what is right. And it seems impossible.

And tell that same Lord Jesus to keep us all from threats of death. For a second day in a row, class was interrupted by a direct threat to me. This time to the tykes as well. By a masked putative bank robber. With a very nasty-looking gun. We were all saved again by Joey Fetter's fast ball. Tell Him we've had enough of this. Please. This, even though the community is getting a lot of fun out of all of these would-be attacks on poor old Father Wolfe.

Luke

FORTY-SIX

Exactly at 11:55 his alarm brought Father Wolfe back to the world of murder and missing boys and motherless kids. He had almost fallen asleep over the computer. Would he need a jacket? Probably not. He had lain—*lie, lay, lain; lay, laid, laid*—how often he had explained the use of that simple yet apparently esoteric word to his classes?—down fully dressed and had slept fitfully.

Quietly down the hall. Easy down the stairs. Into the mailroom. Turn the light on. And there in his box was a ragged piece of lined binder paper. Somewhat soiled in a way that only young males can achieve. The penciled note was brief: The canal side of the Tennis Shack. Now.

The Tennis Shack was south of the Jesuit residence. With a paved school road in between. And south of the Tennis Shack was another paved road, mainly used by maintenance trucks. Further south still, was the cyclone fence and then the gravel road bordering the Arizona Water Service canal.

Out the front door. A quick walk to the north side of the Shack. Around the east side and back to the south side.

FORTY-SEVEN

"Hi, Father." Two voices together.

"God help us." It was so easy to pray these days. "Where have you guys been? How did you get here?"

"Uhuhuh, Father. Leave that to us."

"And you'll have to leave to us how we got this information."

"About the murderer?"

"Yes."

"Why does all this have to be so hush-hush and secret? Can't you unwrap it all to the police and come back? Home? School?"

"We will, Father, when you've put this murderer behind bars for the rest of his days. Right now, it ain't safe." Father Wolfe paused in mental midflight, then forbore to point out that it was *isn't*. And it was not Father Wolfe who was supposed to bring the murderer to justice.

"All right. Tell me what you have me out here for."

"Well."

"We were getting a little bored. And Terry..."

"...remembered that on the last day we were at..."

"...school, Monday, Benjy Wainwright—"

"—his real name is Benjamin, but that name was..."

I know. I have him in class. I have his name on the class roster.

"...so long everybody calls him Benjy."

"Anyway, Benjy had said that he had this new..."

"...really spooky video game."

"Three-dimensional."

"Interactive."

"And we had not so much as heard of it."

"So we decided to visit Benjy last night."

"To try it on for size."

"One tiny pebble was all it took to get him..."

"...to his bedroom window. And three minutes later we..."

"...were in his room."

"But when we met him at the kitchen door, he kept the lights..."

"...off and insisted that we be absolutely silent."

"He told us we hadda be so quiet because he was supposed..."

"...to be studying. And although his mother and grandmother were not home..."

"...his father was visiting with some important friend."

"He had hardly said that when we heard voices..."

"...one of them very angry and one..."

"...very quiet and coaxing."

"So we never even bothered to try the video or turn..."

"...on the lights. And when we silently crept to the wall..."

"...we could hear almost everything they were saying. And..."

"...when we heard the word *murder*, Terry here pulls out his..."

"...recorder."

Father Wolfe found himself fascinated. "Audio tape recorder?"

"Aw, Father, that's old fashioned stuff. Terry pulled out his..."

"...audio digital recorder. We're gonna lend it to you so that..."

"...you can hear the exact words, if you want. But..."

"...right now we're gonna give you the gist of the whole thing and..."

"...we think you'll unnastan why we're so worried."

"After a few minutes we recognized who the two voices were."

"That's metonymy—as you keep telling us, Father."

"The one voice was Gene Wainwright—Benjy's dad. We knew that because Benjy's dad had often talked to us when we visited Benjy."

"The other voice—we're not so sure."

"But it seems to be that new abortion guy over on Mountain and Seventh Street."

"He's that slimy-looking guy that advertises abortions on TV."

They're actually talking in complete sentences!

"Doctor Tear or Cheer or Fear. Something like that."

"Bier?" Father Wolfe offered the correct version.

"Yeah." Could the triplets' memory be trusted if they couldn't remember a simple name?

"It's Wainwright who is doing most of the talking. And he says..."

"...that he had brought Mrs. Wainwright in..."

"...drugged. And the doctor should have done the abortion."

"The Senator wanted the evidence of his horns removed. We didn't unnastan that."

"But that's what he said. Clearly. Because he wanted the evidence of his horns removed."

"Is that clear, Father?"

"Yes. And no." For a moment Father Luke was back in "The Miller's Tale" again.

"Yes, for the evidence. No, for what it means." Well, the good Senator must have something of a decent education if he knew that word. "It was for having his horns removed." The cuckolded husband—whose wife had been unfaithful to him—had horns that everyone except himself could see. "They're what were to be removed."

"What horns, Father?"

"Not now. Sometime I'll explain."

"Yes." Terry obviously didn't understand.

"Wait." Father Wolfe did not want to be toyed with. "You said 'murderer' and now you're saying 'abortion provider.'"

"We didn't finish, Father."

"He also asked why the doctor hadn't done the according-to-plan sloppy job that would have cut an artery and leave the scene so that Mrs. Wainwright could bleed to death."

"So she could die 'an accidental death.'"

Father Wolfe sighed. He felt hugely depressed. "What else did they say?"

"Well, one of them—it sounded like the Senator—said, 'A drink.'"

"Then there were noisy footsteps—sharp heels, I guess..."

"...walking away."

"And then other footsteps coming our way."

"And then we heard a sound like someone banging his head..."

"...into the wall between them and us. And in an angry voice..."

"...he said, 'Revenge *is* sweet. Ignoring me. The—umm—bitch.'"

Barry paused and looked up at Father Wolfe to see how he was taking this earthy jargon.

"And then the same voice said, 'Play me like a yo-yo. And...'"

"'...my satisfaction and left...'"

"'...you, Gene, with the guilt before the law. I'd tell them you went into the operating theater alone before I even touched her.'"

"That was it. If it was Doctor Bier, he moved far enough from the wall so we couldn't hear any more."

"Except for the sound of the hard footsteps again and then the clink of two glasses a few minutes later." Terry wanted it all to be pellucidly clear.

The boys seemed to be right on target. "I'll have to tell the police about this."

"Sure, Father. Just so they don't know where this lead came from."

"That is, you can tell them it came from us."

"But not tell them where we contacted you."

"Or how."

Father Wolfe sighed. He looked out the window at the nets and lines of the tennis courts that glowed eerily in the yellow light of the all-night arc lamps. "While we're at it, how did you know we were going to have a lockdown?"

"Well, Father, like...." Barry hesitated, waiting for Terry to help him.

"We have this scanner."

"It's a radio you can pick up at any electronics store. Like Radios Anonymous. And you can pick up all the police and fire department radio talk. We listen to it all..."

"...the time. We even got ourselves a motorcycle battery so we could run it on twelve volts outside of the regular 110 and outside a car."

Terry looked from Father Wolfe to Barry, and frowned as though Barry was telling the Father too much.

"And we heard them telling about a robbery at the L & D right by Kino. And..."

"...we heard the helicopter pilot telling the police that the guy they were after was on foot and headed toward Kino."

"Now, when you tell the police about all this Wainwright-Bier business..."

"...don't use your cellphone."

"Why not?"

"Well, Father, if the conditions are right, sometimes it's possible to overhear their messages."

He'd have to call Captain Parsons from his room phone in the Jesuit residence. These kids might not know what they were talking about, but it came through loud and strong as reality.

"Yes, I've heard. OK. Need a ride someplace or food or anything?"

"No thanks, Father. We're doing just fine."

"I'm going to tell your parents that you are safe and that I've seen you both and you're OK. They're worried sick, you know. OK?"

Terry looked at Barry. "OK. You must not tell anyone where you saw us."

"But you can tell them we're OK."

Father Wolfe walked back past the front of the Tennis Shack and back to the front door and back up the stairs and very quietly to his room. He wondered if he would be able to get any sleep that night.

Especially after explaining all this to Parsons, only to have the policeman gently but clearly make it plain that Father Wolfe should somehow have gotten the Mohrs to return to school and family. And the real world.

Well, at least all this would have to wait until morning: he had neglected to bring the Captain's home phone number over from his classroom. And when he looked it up, he found it wasn't there. Unlisted. It could wait until morning.

FORTY-EIGHT

"Well, Chris, what brings you here so early on this splendid Thursday morning?"

It was 7:32 the next morning—Thursday. Just as he had expected, he had slept a troubled and unrefreshing sleep last night. And his morning prayer had been distracted: it had seemed impossible to keep his mind on the coming Sunday's Gospel—during the week before he liked to pray over the readings for his homily. So he had prayed over and over again that all would come right out of all this. And offered himself to the Lord Jesus for anything He might want from Luke to make it so. And then he wondered if he was awake enough to really mean what he was saying.

Father Wolfe had unlocked his classroom door, and before he got the door open, Chris Spengle had materialized beside him. Chris was a gangly six-foot-two sophomore whose arms and legs never seemed to fit properly on his broad torso. He had a lean face, bright eyes and a mop of almost platinum-blond hair that was cut short but always seemed in need of a wheat-threshing haircut.

"I wonder if I can take that *Shoeless Joe* test. You know, the one I missed last week when I was sick." He smiled to make sure Father remembered he had been absent for three days the week before.

"Fine, Chris."

He sat down at his desk, unlocked the file drawer in it and pulled out the file labeled *Shoeless*. He wrote Spengle on the top of one of the orange-colored tests and then again on the white page of the essay-question test. "Just boot up any of the computers for that second part of the test."

"Hiya, Father." Tony seemed incapable of saying those words without being enthusiastically loud.

"Good morning, Father." Rita was hand-in-hand with Tony. They were trailed by Larry.

Curious, Father Wolfe looked at Larry. How bright his eyes were when he looked at Rita. It was obvious that he owed her a lot—she had, after all, with her own story of pain and the need to forgive, weaned him from his insistence on killing all baby killers—and that he recognized that she was an exceptionally good woman.

And she certainly was very pretty. And Larry was a very normal male.

But was there anything more than that?

"Hi, Father." Larry smiled his smile that lifted the corners of his small mouth and worked its way up to his eyes and looked into Father Wolfe's eyes to show that they shared the secret of his imprisonment and conversion and pain of loss. And finding God's forgiving peace in confession to Father Atkins. After Rita had brought him to his senses.

"Father, we'd like to proposition you." Tony laughed.

"Well! I hope not!" Father Wolfe mocked shock.

"Oh, it's something good." Tony laughed again. "Rita will explain." And he squeezed her hand and looked at her as though she had just come down from Sinai and had the two tablets in her hands.

"Father, please come with us this coming Saturday when we protest over at Family Freedom." She was at her prettiest when she was serious. "A big bunch of kids are coming from here and Mother Teresa, and we'd get even more if they knew you were taking this time to support them. And even Larry is coming."

Larry. Father Wolfe could see from Larry's pleading look at him that the boy had not been at the clinic in memory since he thought he had murdered his father and had later been released from jail. The memories undoubtedly were too painful.

Jesus, how in the world am I going to find time for this? I'm nowhere near caught up on my paper-correcting. And it will probably take every free moment I have to prepare that test on Agatha Christie's ABC Murders. *And there's the hour Sunday morning to help out at St. Ignatius Loyola next door. How can I spare the time?*

"Sure." He hoped he had said it more brightly than he felt. "What time?"

"Ten."

"You want me to come in my priest clothes or in mufti."

"Mufti?" That was Tony again.

"Yes. The kind of clothes you wear instead of a uniform. Like, my black clothes with the turned-around collar." Where had he picked that expression up? *On the Waterfront* maybe. When the priest with the cauliflower nose–Karl Malden–was talking to Marlon Brando/Terry Malloy.

"Priest clothes would be much better this time, Father." Rita was the first to respond.

"And turned-around collar, Father." And Larry winked as he said it.

And then the three of them were gone.

"Father, did I get a hundred on my objective test, hunh?" Chris had found it impossible to finish the essay before he found out if he had passed and was standing next to Father Wolfe's desk, putting on his anxious-dog-waiting-for-a-snack-from-the-dinner-table act.

"Well, let's take a look."

FORTY-NINE

It was 8:05. Father Wolfe picked up the phone and called Captain Parsons.

"Captain, I have to talk to you soon."

"Fire away."

"But not on the phone. And right away." *Have I said that already?* "If you could get over here to Kino—my classroom—at just about any time—all my classes have writing assignments today, and they will be busy at the computers. But if you want me to come down there, I can make it by about three."

"See you there, Father. As soon as I can. But it probably won't be till 9:30 or so."

"It can wait that long, I guess."

FIFTY

"Mikey, where's your theme topic?" The seniors in period four—the first one today—were writing essays on the class computers. Endeavoring to solve a problem Father Wolfe had presented them with—about *The Picture of Dorian Gray*, the movie based on the classic Oscar Wilde novel.

Mikey—it was surprising that he liked to be called by this diminutive when at 17 years he was already six-foot-four and weighed somewhere around 250 pounds—Richards scrolled up twenty lines on his computer and pointed. It was the last sentence of his introductory paragraph.

"Umm. Right here, Father."

"Make it the second paragraph—just a single sentence—and tighten it up to one main clause." Father Wolfe was walking around the classroom, looking over the shoulder of each student as he worked his way through the essay due by the end of class. And making, he hoped, constructive comments.

There was a loud clearing of a throat, by the door. As soon as Father Wolfe saw that it was Captain Parsons, he quickly walked over. The room was abuzz with the sound of hungry computers.

"Guess you couldn't hear my polite request to come in."

"Sorry about that."

Captain Parsons waved it away like chasing a fly.

"This is very private, Captain. Come out into the hall."

Father looked up and down the corridor to make sure that no one was near enough to hear them. "The Mohr boys have told…"

"Where are those kids?" The Captain was gesturing the way people think only Italians gesture—fluently—here with hands out like wings as though he were ready to take off. And the look on his face included thunder. "Phoned you?"

"No. We met. Shhhshhh." Captain Parsons' voice was much too loud for Father Wolfe's peace of mind. "They made me promise to tell no one. Except you—the police. So I still don't know where they are, but they claim to have a very"—Father Wolfe paused to find the right word—"important piece of information for us." *Us. Wasn't this the Captain's sole responsibility? Had he taken it on?*

Captain Parsons chewed the end of his luxuriant mustache, frustrated. "I'm listening."

"Well, they told me that they had overheard Senator Wainwright and Dr. Aldo Bier talking. And they had heard them say that the MO"—well, where had he come up with that piece of police jargon?—"had been that the Senator would bring Gina—drugged—up to the abattoir. Once there, Bier would do an abortion on her and make it look like an accident that he had wounded her somehow and he could not stop the bleeding. And as a result she was supposed to die. But they wanted no bit of evidence to be found. And that lack of evidence thing they still had not figured out."

"When did they tell you this, Father? You say it wasn't on the phone?"

"No, but I had to promise them I wouldn't tell you how they had found out."

"Well. Well. Well." Captain Parsons stroked his mustache and laughed a little. In spite of his obviously very virile looks, it sounded more like a girl's giggle than anything else. "Well. Well. Well." There it was: déjà vu all over again.

"You knew about this already?"

"No. No. No."

How repetitious was he going to get?

"But there was no abortion, Father. As soon as Gina's body was brought down to forensics—about an hour after you discovered her—Dr. Sands did an immediate autopsy and was surprised to find a baby in her womb and of course very much departed this life. With no support from his mother, he—yes, it's a boy—had no hope of surviving. When she froze they both froze together. He seemed to be about seven months along. Yes. Yes. Yes, I know what you want to ask. Yes, for a baby he bore a striking resemblance to the Senator. Eyes and nose. The Greek nose was a dead giveaway. I know. I know. I know, Senator Wainwright isn't Greek. But if you will reflect on his face for just a moment you will remember that he has a very prominent nose. Sharp like a mountain. Like Hunters' Peak up there at the north end of Seventh. And the eyes. That deep-ocean blue. And just a little too far apart."

FIFTY-ONE

"Skye, what are you doing?" It was the first period on the schedule, the one just before lunch since this was Thursday. The sophomores had hardly sat down after the prayer. Skyler Blue was going from desk to desk with his cap inverted in his hand before himself.

"We're taking up a collection."

"A collection." It was a statement framed in wonder. "Umm—may I ask what for?"

"Sarcasm, no sarcasm, Father." It was Skye again.

"We were just taking up a collection for Joel Stearman's new tie. We pretty much turned it into a rag when we used it for a rope to tie Harold Gribbs' hands."

"And he's got to have the official Kino school tie at all our mandatory dress-code Masses and other functions." Larry Heinlein liked to make sure that everyone understood reality from his point of view.

"So if everybody chips in a whopping twenty cents, with the thirty-five of us, that comes to $7.00—enough for Joel to buy a new tie and a couple of Cokes at the Snackeree to assuage his pain. That is, if everyone comes up with the massive amount of twenty cents." And he glared at Herman Sprout. Undoubtedly Herman had failed to render his part of the deal.

"OK. And while you're doing that, why don't we do a little memory? Terry, do you want to take us for a ride in that second stanza of 'Sam Magee'?"

"Why sure, Father." Terry Mahan climbed out of his desk with the aplomb of a king majestically rising to his feet to proclaim a new edict for his vassals.

"Now, Sam Magee was from Tennessee,
  where the cotton blooms and blows.
Why he left his home in the South to roam
  round the Pole God only knows.
He was always cold, but the land of gold
  seemed to hold him like a spell,
Though he'd often say in his homely way
  that 'he'd sooner live in hell.'"

"Father, shouldn't that be 'only God knows'? God really could be doing a lot of other things besides only knowing." Hans Andfeet loved to let the class know how deeply he understood the English language.

"We made enough—$6—for Joel to buy himself a new tie and a Coke."

"Excellent, Skye. Right on, Hans. You're quite correct. But if you will listen to the line your way, you will see that it interrupts the meter. Undoubtedly that's why Robert Service took that liberty."

The class had scarcely finished their turn at reciting when the bell rang.

FIFTY-TWO

As the bell rang to end the school day, a very quiet and very dark small man had hesitantly appeared at the doorway.

Father Wolfe had planned to visit Mr. and Mrs. Mohr right after school to tell them that their sons were safe. Even though he couldn't tell them where they were. Or use the telephone to do this.

"Father, my name Mohandas Patchavar. I from India. Please excuse." And he smiled a huge and warm and toothy smile on his very round, dark face.

Well, he looks like Kipling's Gunga Din, all right. He is very dark. But he is wearing a lot more in the clothes line.

Amazing that there was not the shred of an accent even if the syntax was fractured. "Are you the father of Spencer?"

Mohandas nodded a happy yes. "Real Psyllium. American Spencer." He opened his hands in front of him and displayed an embarrassed look. Clearly the boy was to be an American with an American name. Not Indian here.

"Does he well? Books?" The happy smile again.

"Very well. Spencer is one of the best students in the class. Does he have any little brothers that you will send to us here at Kino soon?"

"No." And Mohandas shrunk a little in his clothes. "Spencer only. Mother no children." His open palm that waved to his side added "more" to the "no."

"Father." Mohandas paused and looked down at his hands in his lap. "I have." And again the gesture. "Say."

"More to tell me?"

"Yes. More. Thank you." His eyes the color of his skin flashed gratitude for a moment on Father Wolfe's face. "I no know who tell. Afraid. You tell no"— Mohandas paused and shook his head in the effort to recollect—"people?"

People. Does he mean police? What was this all about? "Only the police if they need to be informed. And they always try to avoid naming the innocent individual's name in the newspapers."

"OK."

"What's the trouble?"

"Wife Indira and I no legal. False passports. Afraid kick out."

"Why 'kick out,' Mohandas?" Even in his impatience, Father Luke had to slow everything down, trying to be as gentle as he could.

"Bad acts. And bad see."

"You've done something bad and you've witnessed something criminal. And you are afraid that the police will put you in bad with the immigration people and send you back to India?"

"Yes." Mohandas' eyes looked brightly and happily on Father Wolfe for a moment and then went back to staring sadly at the floor.

"Wife Indira I work doctor office. Gynocolo—. Seven and Mountain. We see woman night die."

"Oh, my God!" It was Father Wolfe's most earnest prayer of the day.

"We afraid tell before. But heart"—he gestured an enthusiastical circle in front of his chest—"no allow speak. Pain."

And for the next twenty minutes with garbled words, broken sentences and eloquent gestures, he explained what he had come to tell Father Wolfe.

Finally, his open palms made it clear that he had run dry.

"See Father. Again." And he moved quickly and noiselessly out the door.

FIFTY-THREE

"Mrs. Mohr, this is Father Wolfe." Father Wolfe was in his room at the Jesuit house—using the "safe" phone—according to the "twins."

"Yes, Father." Her voice was husky. Was she sobbing?

"Is Mr. Mohr there with you?"

"No, Father. He doesn't usually get home until 5:30 or 6:00."

"May I come over then? I have some good news for both of you."

FIFTY-FOUR

Father Wolfe parked the Neon in front of the neat grass carpeting every corner of the front yard and garnished with a plethora of ground cover color, all guarded by the stately palm.

He wanted to pull up in the driveway behind the Schwartz truck. "Park it in the street," they had said. So he did.

She was holding the screen door partly ajar as he came up the three steps. And opened it wide for him.

Middle, late thirties, she was still as slim as a high school girl. And if she had not been so worried about her sons, she would probably have smiled. "Good afternoon, Father. I'm Sharon Mohr. This is my husband Neil." He had the same little-boy looks of the "twins," but weather-toughened and a little longer in the jowls.

"Sit down, Father. Coffee?"

"Or a wee nip?" In spite of his sadness, Neil's voice took on a Gaelic ring. Was Neil from the auld sod? His brogue seemed particularly authentic.

"No, thank you. I just came over to tell you that your boys are safe."

Instantly Sharon was giving Father Luke an enthusiastic bear-hug—surprisingly strong for so slight a woman, the warmest he could remember. "Thank God." Mrs. Mohr sank down into the cushioned chair next to her. And just let the tears come. A river.

And then Neil was shaking his hand as though he wanted it to fall off. "Oh, Father." More shaking. "It's so good to hear you say that."

Suddenly Mary was in the room. You couldn't mistake that she was the third member of the triplets. Save that her hair was longer. And she was a healthy-looking teen-age girl. But skinny the way the ads said they were all supposed to look. Or the store mannequins.

"Hullo, Father." She reached out her hand. "I'm Mary." She had a very nice smile.

"I would have suspected as much."

"They've told me all about you."

"Good things, I hope." Luke looked down into her eyes to see how she would take that.

"I have seen them both. And they look healthy and fit. But they don't want anyone to know where they are. And they insist that everything is all right with them: they don't need anything—nor food nor clothes nor transportation."

Mary smiled a knowing smile at that. Had the "twins" been keeping her abreast of things?

"And they wanted you to know this. And that you shouldn't worry. And that they will be back soon."

"Oh, Father." Sharon was off the sofa and was giving Father Wolfe another ecstatic hug.

Neil reached out his hand once again. "Thank you, Father. Thank you."

FIFTY-FIVE

Chollie,

We're back to square one. Yes, it's Thursday night. What happened? Are the kids right? They insist that they know that the murderer was Dr. Bier. And the Senator himself had cooperated. They said they had heard them talking at the Senator's house—courtesy of their interest in Benjy's computer game they were there to see. Or did they misunderstand what these two people were talking about? Did they mistakenly identify them? And if these two guys were who the kids thought they were, had that been an original plan—that they both cooperated in a murder and then one of them had backed out? And why would the Senator want to murder his beautiful wife that everyone says he was madly in love with? Even if she had been unfaithful to him. And she had, of course, insisted that she had always been faithful and true to her I do.

Grab the Holy Spirit by the lapels and tell Him we need to find out how those boys are avoiding us and how to get them back.

It would be a great starter for peace and quiet to find Gina's murderer.

And then there was my afternoon visitor.

Well, you had better make louder noises to the Lord Jesus to straighten out all this mess.

The father of one of my students visited me today to ask about his son's progress. Boy is doing wonderfully well.

And then—Mohandas Patchavar is his name—he proceeded to tell me that he and his wife, Indira, are illegal immigrants from India. Why illegal, I am not sure: I suspect it's because of forged passports.

More important, they help out at the abattoir at Seventh and Mountain. It was the only place they could find that would hire them. No friends. No source of money. Living in and on the dream of our freedom. They seemed to think it was a gynecologist's office. Really? Or to salve their consciences?

And they were there the night Gina Wainwright was brought in.

And they were the ones who put her bloody body in the back of the Schwartz ice cream truck.

Mohandas has a lot of trouble with the English language, but what he had to tell was pretty clear. According to him Gene Wainwright drives up and carries his wife's body—over his shoulder, as Mohandas graphically demonstrated—upstairs to Doctor Bier's operating theater. She doesn't look dead. She looks as though she were sleeping. Or drugged. The doctor starts to put on his surgical outfit when he gets into a fierce argument with the Senator. What seemed to end things was when the good doctor very ironically almost shouts: "I ain't gonna take no murder rap for doing your dirty work for you." I know, I know, Mohandas was difficult to understand, but by repeating it differently several times, he made what the unhappy doctor said very clear. "You can cover your own ass for yourself!" Mohandas swept his hand across his backside to get that one across. "Do you think I'm a murderer?" Irony here, pretty heavy-handed, hunh?

When the doctor comes out of the theater to take off his smock and hat and gloves—or whatever they wear for their fun and games—Gene goes into the theater, even though Bier tells him in a clear but not loud voice to stay out of there. For just a minute or so, and they leave, the both of them arguing vehemently—that was not his word, but he made it very plain by his gestures. He thought they were heading out to the all-night bar kitty-corner from the Family Freedom place. To come to some conclusion to their differences. And to get stiffened up to do the job: Mohandas says the doctor seldom did an operation when he was completely sober. And as they leave, the doctor tells Mohandas and his wife not to touch nothing nohow—the lady is just asleep.

Anyway—hey, this is getting long, isn't it?—they had hardly left when a black car pulls into the parking place with its lights off. The Patchavars could see this because they had left the operating theater to go to their coffee room which was still—still, because much of the clinic had been changed by Doctor Bier since the murder of Doctor Curtland—on the second floor and on the west side of the building around the corner from the cutting room.

They wait for someone to ring the bell, or knock or something. It was way after hours when the doctor had been about to do his business. Nothing. Only after a bit they heard a kind of sawing sound. But very soft. Was someone cutting his way in? Later Mohandas figured what they heard might have been a credit card working the bolt on the outer door. Wanting to keep as low a profile as possible because of their citizenship status, they slowly and silently tiptoe from the coffee room toward the surgery room. And there they see someone—it was impossible to determine if it was man or a woman—Mohandas seemed to think it walked like a woman, although the size of the coat made any kind of gender identification impossible. And it was a Columbo coat. Mohandas didn't call it that. What he said was, "TV. Bad eye. Columbo." He gestured a garment that went from neck to calf, had pockets, a collar. Trench coat—Mohandas mimicked a soldier firing a rifle with difficulty over the edge of a trench. A little too long. They could see little or nothing of the person wearing it. Except that a bit of light hair was visible in the light from the street. It was either very blonde or white: it was just a snatch of a look as the intruder was silently leaving.

And again the car seemed to be black. This time they looked more carefully. It seemed to be small. But they could glean no license numbers—the lights were off until it was far down the block.

FIFTY-SIX

I phoned Captain Parsons immediately, of course. He was a little surprised by all this. But from Mohandas' description of the coat, Parsons wondered out loud that that sounded just like the coat Gina's mother often wore during the winter when the Senator wanted a press conference with a large entourage of intelligent and beautiful people. And she does have that shock of white hair on the left side, just where the Patchavars would have seen it. Sad. She seemed like such a good woman.

Captain Parsons said this should be enough reason to get a search warrant for the Senator's residence—to see what they could dig up in the way of drugs.

But before that I told him that Mohandas and his wife, after wondering what the intruder wanted, went to the operating theater only to find to their horror that Gina was soaked in blood. And when they tried to find a pulse in her neck and found none, they concluded that she was very dead. And they would be blamed. That was their fear. What should they do? Was there some way of getting rid of the body? They looked out the window, and there behind the building was a huge ice cream truck. They read the two-foot-high letters Schwartz *and* Ice Cream *on the back side. Its back door slightly ajar. A freezer. A place to rid themselves of the body. Like a madman—Mohandas was tearing his hair as he said, "Free. Safe?" As he told me this, his eyes wild—he picked up the bloody body, raced with it down the back stairs, put the body in the truck, raced back up again, stripped, threw his bloody clothes into the wash machine and put on a clean outfit. You would have been as fascinated as I was to see him intersperse his few words with graphic gestures to communicate all this.*

When the doctor returned an hour and a half later, they told him that Gina had awakened, called a taxi and left. The doctor was under the affluence of too much incahol—as they say in your local bar—to do much more than nod agreement and tell them to go home. Apparently he had convinced Gene that he would not do the abortion. Or at another time. Or was that even what this was all about?

But why? Did he decide there was nothing in it for himself?

And then I went over to the pretty Mohr house. And told his parents and his sister that they were safe. It would have been oh-so-good to be able to tell them more. But I knew hardly more than that myself. Save for the murder details.

Luke

FIFTY-SEVEN

Father Wolfe woke up. Even before he opened his eyes, he knew what had been bothering him about the triplets' phone calls. The street noise he had heard behind them on the phone was precisely the same street noise he was hearing with his other ear. Clearly, they must be someplace close.

And if that was true, then this was the best time to check out every local possibility.

The alarm winked from 1:37 to 1:38. He sighed. Best to get this over with. Now. He got up, threw on a shirt and walking shorts and shoes, grabbed his flashlight and quietly headed for the stairs.

Where should he start?

Jesuit garden? Behind the Tennis Shack? How about behind those enormous canisters the city had left at the far end of the tennis courts for recycling paper?

He quietly opened the arcadia door at the end of the conference room, tiptoed up the stairs and quietly started to follow the garden wall.

When he came to the first corner, there they were. Comfortable and happily curled up, each in his sleeping bag.

Well, that was easy.

Wake them now? Better. Put an end to this insanity.

"Barry, Terry, wake up." He was leaning over them where their heads almost met.

"Oh, hi, Father."

"Father."

It was as though they had met in front of Father Wolfe's classroom and were going to pass the time of day.

"What are you two doing out here?"

"Well. It's a long story and..."

"Be careful of the mother mallard and her three little ones in their nest right behind you. We think she came over from the canal to have her chicks here—safe and sound. But we've had trouble keeping the rapacious cats away."

Hey, they're picking up a pretty sophisticated vocabulary.

"Right now we're hungry. Larry looked at his watch. "Right about..."

"...now we usually go in and get something to eat."

"Where?"

"In the Jesuit kitchen."

"Of course. Where else?" *No sarcasm, now, Father.*

FIFTY-EIGHT

In the kitchen the two boys went to the fridge and the freezer and pulled out whatever seemed enticing, put whatever needed to be heated into the microwave.

"Can we get you a beer or something, Father? Bit of this nice-looking bratwurst that must be left over from supper?"

"Sure. Why not?" *No sarcasm now, Luke.* Father Wolfe hoped his tone of voice had not betrayed the huge irony of the situation.

"Well, I guess you would like to know what's going on."

They were sitting at the big kitchen table. The kids were into the leftover-from-supper lasagna and brats and green beans and lettuce-and-tomato salad. Father Wolfe contented himself with a Miller's Lite and a brat embraced by two slices of rye bread. And wondered a little about two adolescents without any prompting eating a well-balanced meal. Ask them later. Not now.

"Well, yes, I would." Father laughed a little and looked first at one and then the other. *How ingenuous are they?*

"Like, where should we start?" That was Terry.

"How 'bout with the day we told you about finding..."

"...the body? And you were going to phone the police and we..."

"...disappeared." Barry looked reproachfully at Father. "And you promised not to tell anyone."

"No, Barry, you never gave me a chance to promise anything."

Barry was obviously surprised by this idea and looked across at Terry to see if this was going down as easily as the bratwurst. As their eyes met, they both clearly signaled to one another that it was all right.

"But now you have to promise..."

"...us that none of this—none of this..."

"...will go any further. Or..."

"...we can't tell you any more."

Father Wolfe carefully studied his own bratwurst as he tried to mask by apparent insouciance his awareness of what was going on. But he knew he was trapped.

"OK. I promise."

FIFTY-NINE

"See. We figgered the worst that could happen was that..."

"...the Dean would suspend us." Barry took a huge gulp from his can of Coke.

"We knew you would tell Mom and Dad that we were OK."

"It worried us that Mom and Dad couldn't know that for a while, but what else could we do?"

"And if the police were nettled"—he paused to look up from his lasagna at Father Luke to be sure Father remembered that it was a vocabulary word from class that he was using—"well, the worst that could happen was that some old judge would, like, give us a good talking to."

Father Wolfe deposited the half-empty glass of beer on the table and reached up to straighten the few strands of his white hair. *If he doesn't also fine your parents the police-search costs.*

"And we figgered that the closer we got to you or home the less likely..."

"...anyone would think to look for us here. And we called our sister, Mary, and got her promise..." It was Terry this time who gave Father Luke a look of disappointment for not having kept his expected promise of secrecy. The one that he had pointed out that he had never made. "...to bring us sleeping bags. She threw them over the wall. We didn't need much else."

"Except a couple of her wigs."

"We came in here at night for food. We got to like the way you guys eat." That was obvious from the way Barry was massaging his gullet with everything in sight. "Maybe we'll become Jesuits so we can chow down this way all the time."

Father Wolfe took another bite of what little was left of his rye and brat, filled his glass from the can and took another sip of the Miller's. He laughed quietly. *Well, God could start with very faulty motivation and turn it into service for his kingdom.*

In a moment he was back in San Francisco—fifty, sixty years ago—when with the help of Janey Peers' prayers and bringing him to Mass with her every day he had decided that he was going to do the best thing he could with his life. Childish reason for becoming a priest. But the seminary emphasis on prayer and the sacraments had shifted that to the desire to serve Jesus Christ's cause with everything he had. He knew it wasn't much. But, still, it was everything he had to offer.

SIXTY

“We almost took the car keys from the upstairs bulletin board.”

“But we figgered you guys might not be too happy about that.”

“Like insurance?” Terry lifted his eyes off his almost empty plate to confirm from Father Wolfe’s expression the maturity of that decision.

Father Wolfe’s only response was to look steadily at him. With a look of wonder.

“But the best was yet to come.” *How much further could they go with this ruse?*

“We waltzed out of here decorated with the wigs and the black T-shirts Mary—our sister, remember?—hustled from somewhere.”

Did they think I am so ancient that I cannot remember that their sister’s name is Mary for a few minutes?

“And started wandering around town in the daylight. Nobody took notice of us dudes who were hookeying it.” Barry laughed. And got very much caught up in brushing a small piece of lettuce off the front of his shirt.

“Irony.” Terry smiled.

“Which we were.”

“And just yesterday we caught up with Benjy Wainwright in the school parking lot. Made him promise not to betray us. And we were off.”

“The Dean saw us from across the parking lot. And looked as though he recognized us from somewhere. But he didn’t do anything. I guess he just couldn’t place us—with our wigs and all.”

"And gave it up. And Benjy drove us to his home. It's a palace. This time no one was home. So we wandered all over the place."

"No one at all."

"Even into his father and mother's room. And his grandma's."

"And the room of the live-in lady that Benjy says does all the household chores, from cooking to cleaning." Clearly they were talking about Allie Carpenter.

"We thought maybe we shouldn't be doing that. But it was..."

"...Benjy's idea anyway."

"And that's where Benjy was surprised as he picked up six prescription pill boxes in the cooking lady's apartment."

"But the name on the pill containers was Henrietta Goodwin, Benjy's great-grandmother. It seemed, like, strange."

"That's not the au pair's name—is that the right word, Father?"

Where have they been gleaning all these esoteric words? Au pair *was certainly not one of their class vocabulary words.*

"Close enough."

"It's Allie Carpenter."

Father Wolfe wondered aloud where all this was going.

"It dint seem to be going anywhere. So we let it hang out to dry." Then Terry finished off his large bowl of Dreyer's Pralines and Cream in silence.

SIXTY-ONE

Benjy's grandmother, Marie Goodwin, was waiting for Father Wolfe when he returned to the sacristy after the 6:30 Mass at St. Ignatius on Friday morning.

"I'm glad you said Mass at this time, Father."

"Father Walsh came down with a terrible cold yesterday. And Father Pastor Jones asked me to come over before school and help out."

"Saves me trying to find you during school hours."

Father Wolfe slipped the chasuble over his head and started to hang it in the closet. "Why did you want to find me?" It came out muffled. He hung the stole on the empty peg inside the closet door.

"I don't know if I told you my mother died, Father. I wanted you to say Mass for her, but I got caught up in so many other things." She started to cry. Weakly. Quietly.

"I'm sorry. I will be happy to say that Mass tomorrow morning, Marie. With God there is no time. So it will be just as if I were saying it the moment after she died. But it probably won't be here in the church."

"That's all right."

"Did she die here in Phoenix?"

"No, Father. Santa Monica. California. Surprise heart attack. Six months. She was getting along—but she could still do for herself, and her mind was clear. She seems to have dropped dead in her kitchen while she was getting her supper ready. And was not found till the day after when a friend came over to see her and was surprised to find her car in the driveway and got no response from the bell and heavy knocking.

"I was back there most of that week. Funeral. She had a lot of friends, clearly. Sorting her few things out. Will. Clothes. Medicines."

"I understand. My mother died in a nursing home a few years ago after a long bout of illness. I understand." Father Wolfe's voice went muffled again as he slipped the white alb over his head.

"But a surprising thing happened. Just then Gina had to come to Los Angeles.

"I met her arriving on Southwest at LAX. She had phoned me from here and asked that I pick her up. She was there to try to build a base for helping her blind kids here in Phoenix and spreading the word to others about what they could do in their own locale. And she stayed with me at my mother's place. And she helped me with sending Mother's things to St. Vincent de Paul. It was a great help to have her there. She patiently stayed with me there the whole time. And I found it such a blessing to be near her that I went to all of her talks.

"Interestingly enough, after one of her speeches—the audience had stood and clapped enthusiastically for ever so long—Jerry Harris came up and congratulated her on the talk, said he was in town for Beckmann and Collier—is that the right name?—and had read in the paper about her coming talk, thanked her again for her help and advice to see you, Father, and was on his merry way.

"Gina obviously likes this candid young Catholic. With both hands she shook his hand, and gave him that warm, sweet trademark smile she livens—well, livened—the world with for all of us."

"That wasn't the 'surprising thing,' was it?" Father Wolfe was not to be sidetracked.

"Oh no. That's just warm-hearted Gina. What was peculiar was that with the few things I brought back from mother's were the pill containers of coumadin—you know, the medicine to thin your blood if there is any danger of a stroke present. Her doctor had her taking it and, apparently, he had written up the prescription for her to get six refills. She had filled that prescription right away—so she wouldn't have to go back and back and back to the pharmacist for those refills. I'm somehow sure he and she shouldn't have done that. But in a way it was merciful to an old lady who now wouldn't have to be going back to the pharmacy.

"I brought them back with me since my doctor—you know, that nice Doctor Morgan over on 35th—you had him in class, didn't you, Father?—had prescribed this for me—guess it runs in the fambly—so I figgered I could save a little money by bringing them back for myself."

Father Wolfe didn't want to look up at the clock on the sacristy wall. He should be over in his classroom in just a few minutes, he supposed. So he wouldn't stop her by suggesting somehow *FAM-lee* for *fambly* and *FIG-yoord* for *figgered.* He had finished shrugging out of his alb and had it ready in hand. Marie's openness and vivacity made her easy to listen to.

"I put the coumadin away in my handkerchief drawer, down underneath everything else. And didn't think about it until this morning when I noticed my regular supply was getting low. I went to the drawer to discover that all six pill vials were gone. ”

“I’m sorry you lost all that money. When we get older we tend to get forgetful.”

“I might be older.” Marie stiffened slightly. “And I do tend to forget more often. But I know I put the filled vials in that drawer. I distinctly remember mentioning it to Gina and pointing out that every time I took one of those pills I would be reminded to pray for Mom.

“Father, her name is Henrietta—Henrietta Goodwin—when you say that Mass for her.”

SIXTY-TWO

Just before his free period, second period in the day today—Friday—his prep period, but why they called it that since most of the teachers sat in the teachers' lounge and relaxed with a cup of coffee and water-cooler chatter, although that may well have been the best way to really prepare for the rest of the day—his cell phone had gurgled, and it was Mrs. Amy Bates asking him to come as soon as possible to see Principal Sloan.

"Good morning, Father." Father Luke had taken only a few minutes to get from the lounge to the principal's office.

"How are things going? Is our local detective finding the missing boys?" And he smiled his rather toothy smile. Father Wolfe immediately saw that something more than a pleasant little chat was coming.

"There's nothing more to tell you, Gerry." He had promised Terry and Barry, hadn't he? "The police right now hold out little hope of finding them. The *Observer* has publicly worried that the boys have been murdered and hidden. Or that they have just gone off to become street kids somewhere. They wondered if they have set out to live with their grandmother in Flagstaff. But there was no help from any of these leads. Apparently no one has seen any sign of them. None, whatsoever. Or if they have, they're not telling. Captain Parsons keeps me abreast of their drama."

Father Luke was surprised at how adroit he had been at one and the same time telling the truth and keeping it hidden. Equivocation. Mental reservation. Amphibology. That "jesuitical" way to cover apparent lying. But which meant that if the listener had no right to know, it is quite all right to say something with two or more possible meanings from which the listener can get the real meaning but more probably get the other meaning.

Father Sloan shook his head sadly and then, grasping the right lens of his large glasses, lifted them a little higher on his nose. "Father, I noticed that you were not at Rudy Carlton's Blackboard class yestidday—your computer versatility updating, you know."

Father Wolfe was taken back thirty-nine—forty?—years to that classroom when Father Sloan was Gerry Sloan, sophomore. They were critically reading *Julius Caesar*, and Father Wolfe had asked Gerry to take the part of Antony. Gerry had taken on the part enthusiastically and right now was right in the middle of Antony's famous speech.

> But yestidday the word of Caesar might
> Have stood against the world. Now lies he there
> And none so poor to do him reverence.

"Gerry, that word is YES-ter-day." Father Wolfe had mouthed it very clearly to emphasize the usual pronunciation that differed from the tight lips—was it a San Francisco variant emigrated to Phoenix?

"Yes, Father. Yestidday." The class laughed a little.

"Let's try that again, Ger. In the United States—in Arizona—today, we say YES-ter-day. And that 'ter' rhymes with 'fur.' As in 'Fuzzy Wuzzy,' the bear without any. Want to try that again?"

"That's what I said, Father. Yestidday." Father Wolfe looked down and saw that Gerry was red in the face with confusion. The class finally quieted down from its maniacal laughter. "Let's move on." It had seemed better not to try again.

But right now he was in Principal Sloan's office. And now he felt ashamed for having humiliated Gerry—no matter how good his didactic intentions had been. "That's right, Ger."

"I know there was no mandate to be there, but don't you think that you of all the teachers—more than any of the other teachers—should have attended?" Father Sloan looked up into Father Wolfe's face with his guileless stare. "After all, you are the oldest teacher here and from that kind of experience should be encouraging all of us to take on the new ways. We should all become cyber-perfect. That's what Rudy's efforts are aimed at."

"Gerry, I would have been there. But a concerned parent wanted to talk."

"You could have asked her to come back later."

"Him, Ger. And he seemed much too worried and distraught to be put off." He would have to be careful not to implicate Mohandas Patchavar. "Besides, I attended Rudy Vandervogel's explanation—three months or so ago."

Father Sloan looked at Father Wolfe as though he had known this all along. "And did you start using this great tool with your classes?"

"No, Gerry. I must admit I did not."

Father Sloan just waited, his eyes peering through the big glasses at Father Luke's face.

"But when I asked Rudy what the point of Blackboard was, he gave me the obvious answer: this was a neat and modern way of keeping up contact with our students. After class is over and a student gets an idea about what went on in class, he can computerly offer his comments to not only the teacher but to his fellow classmates as well. Especially is this a great idea for the nebbish student who, for one reason or another, is slow to make comments in class. When I asked him how the teacher could tell whether the boy's message had come from the student or one of his parents or his girlfriend or an older brother, Rudy told me that the teacher would be able to tell from what he had learned of the student's ability to think in class. I suggested that if the boy had said little, the teacher would have no criteria for that judgment.

"And then he talked about the new software he had installed in the school's system—software designed to ferret out of a student's writing any quoting from the Internet. But he never did resolve the girl friend difficulty."

Father Sloan cleared his throat and looked blankly at Father Wolfe.

"And besides, I do not understand how a teacher—especially an English teacher—can field all of these lucubrations and return his comments on them either via computer before the next day's class or the next day in the classroom. As it is, most of us English teachers will tell you we cannot keep up with the paper correcting we already must do."

"Well, I do wish you'd see yourself at more of these awakenings for the teachers. We must never become atrophied. Change. Change. Change."

Father Wolfe was reminded of his sharp-eyed and -edged rational psychology teacher—of many years ago—who had been insistent in reminding the students: *Le plus le change, le plus le meme*—things just don't change that much.

But this did not seem like the time to bring it up.

Father Sloan adjusted his glasses once more.

Father Wolfe touched the few white strands on his head. And figured that the whole matter was better left alone. Run with Father Blazer's trust in Father Sloan's ability as an outstanding principal.

SIXTY-THREE

The bell had just rung. It was the last period of the last day of the week. And the seniors were understandably itchy. To have it all bundled up and finished for another week.

Father Wolfe was standing with his back to the open door. Before he could tell the class to stand up for their prayer, a voice behind him said, "Excuse me, Father." It was low and strained. Instead of moving out of the way, Father Wolfe turned around to see Scott Anderson standing there, head down, his face awash with tears. And his button nose was dripping—to add to the flood.

"Harry, bring me my box of Kleenex." Father Wolfe gently took Scott by the shoulder and moved him out of the doorway.

"What's the trouble?"

The boy suppressed a sob. And the waters were loosed even more.

Were they grief? Joy? Release? Yes, the teen-age male could cry. "I'll be all right."

"Scott, what's the trouble?"

When Harry came with the tissues, Father Wolfe tried to shield Scott from him. "Thanks, Harry."

"At lunch yesterday, I got into a fight. In the Mall. With this ***<u>HUGE</u>***"—he underscored it and italicized it and bolded it and capitalized it—"senior. Stranger. Dunno why I had never seen him before. Later I find out his name is Jeff Springer."

"Why?"

"Because he called my sister an"—he looked up through the tears into Father Wolfe's eyes—"unprintable name."

"Why?"

"Don't know. I was walking across the mall"—he made a throwaway open-handed gesture toward the east—"to buy a burrito at the Snackeree, when I hear this voice saying this word. And my sister's name. She's a junior at Mother Teresa, Father. He was looking straight at me."

"And you—?"

"I see now that I shouldn't have. But he looked straight at me and repeated it. In my face! I lost it. Father, my sister may not be perfect, but she's the goodest, kindest, holiest person you would care to meet. And she's not sleeping around—like he said."

"Yes, I met your sister at the Valentine's Day dance when I was prefecting." And the brief meeting said very much the same thing Scott was saying now.

"I'm a lot shorter than he is, but I started hitting at any part of him I could find. And that's when I got this shiner." He looked up at Father again to see if he could see it.

Too bad about the class. This was a lot more important right now.

"Well, his buddies pulled us apart, and Mr. Finney—I guess he was monitoring the Mall—was right there to take me to the Dean. After all, I had started the swinging. And right after school the Dean and his Discipline Board decided after they had talked to Springer and his buddies—they made it all sound like it was all my fault and I just liked to pick on other guys for no reason at all. I hadda sit there outside the room after I had made my speech, waiting for them to make up their minds. And after what must have been a half hour, the Dean came out to tell me that I was to leave Kino. Permanently."

"You must have had a bad night."

"Awful. And I just couldn't tell Mom and Dad. When I told Sis, she didn't say a word—just hugged me and kissed me and cried all over me."

"I don't understand. Why are you still here now?"

"That's why I'm late, Father. I figured I'd tell my folks later when I had a handle on all this. I figured I'd come to school with my carpool and see my buddies here and pick up my books. Father, I really like—love this place and the guys I have come to know here and you teachers that seem to be so concerned about us—even if some of them do get a little boring sometimes.

"I hung around with the guys at Break, and told them what was going on. And somehow Father Sloan got wind that I was around. He sent for me. And asked me to tell him what had happened. I did. I guess he had been talking to those seniors who lied. And to some of you guys.

"And then he said he had rescinded—is that the word, Father?—"

"Sounds like it."

"—the decision of the Discipline Board. Something he said he had not done in five years. And that I was back in school and should go to class."

"Well, Scott, I'm certainly glad you're still with us." Father Wolfe smiled at the boy. Scott had always been hard-working, open and friendly. Something really awry if the witnesses were right. "Would you like to sit out here for a while until you get this under control? We'll bring one of the desks out here for you."

"I'm OK now, Father." He smiled and, cradling the tissues box in his left arm, walked back into class. For a few moments the class was quiet when they saw his tear-stained face. And then they started talking again.

Yes, Blazer was right. There's something in Sloan I have been missing. Is my opinion of him based on when I had him class? On his constantly pushing me? On his stiff demeanor? This whole thing with Scott was the act of a gentle, loving father. Lord, give me a handle on my denigrating spirit about our kindly principal.

"All right, guys, let's say the prayer."

SIXTY-FOUR

It was Saturday morning. And in spite of the drizzle—the rare form of sun-relief afforded Phoenicians who viewed their drought-bringing sun with a love-hate relationship—Rita and Tony and Larry and Father Wolfe had joined the hundred or so other protesters—many more than usual. Jessica Sommers—the informal secretary for the very large number of pro-life people in the Valley—had organized a phone crusade, urging as many as she could to phone others, pointing out that it was important to see what Senator Wainwright had to say about his new pro-choice stand and what, if anything, they could do about it. The self-confident Senator had found out about the bigger-than-usual prayer-rally and apparently thought his speechifying would change their attitude.

Even Father Sloan was there. He had smiled at Father Luke as they passed while saying the Rosary. And his smile seemed to say that this rally was all his idea and that he was very pleased with the turn-out.

Why must I always think malicious thoughts about him? After all, I now see there's a completely different and deeper and more human side to him than I have ever seen before.

They had been praying the Rosary and other prayers—many spontaneous with the help of a bullhorn Jessica had brought—while they walked back and forth in front of and around the corner and back in front of the Family Freedom building.

In a distracted moment, Father Wolfe noticed that Lyda Lott and her sidecar photographer were up on the second floor to the right of the entrance door. Clearly, the Senator wanted to make this a dramatic occasion.

And in another distracted moment he saw Captain Oscar Parsons standing just off to one side of the Rosary-praying group. With him were Lieutenant Higgins and four other uniformed policemen—one of them, sure enough, was carrot-red-haired Sergeant Amy Duchesne. Father Wolfe warmed at the memory that she had been especially kindly and helpful when he had visited Larry Curtland in jail.

Father Wolfe stepped out of line. "Oscar, what are you and your friends doing here? I didn't know you were pro-life. But you're not praying."

"I am very pro-life, Father—if my mother hadn't been pro-life, I wouldn't be here. But we're here on official business. And in that capacity we cannot take sides. When we were alerted that the Senator planned to speak, we were afraid his speech might cause some kind of trouble." He carefully brushed his finger down over his already straight mustache.

"My friends." It was the Senator at the microphone on the balcony overlooking the parking lot. He was so loud that it collapsed the sound of the praying. And Lyda's side-kick Sarah had her camera focused on him.

"Who's he kidding?" Tony Santos' stage-whisper was louder than many people's shout. "With his championing pro-choice and all of us pro-lifers out here?" The football lineman in him was not to be intimidated.

The Senator had probably heard Tony's challenge. But if he had, he ignored it.

"I want to welcome all of you here today." No doubt about it, the Senator has a marvelous voice and a great delivery of the goods. Poise. Cachet. Presence. JFK charisma.

And suddenly from somewhere up above him—and apparently above the main door right above the stairs on the second floor—came a deep rumbling voice. Like an idling jet engine with articulation.

"Senator Eugene Wainwright..."—and without even a nanosecond pause from up above the Senator's right on the opposite end of the porch—"...you murdered your wife Regina Wainwright in the early morning hours..."—and then from the other aerie—"... of Monday, March Tenth." Now it sounded more like thunder—although the words were clear enough. And all of them were somehow almost capitalized.

Just where the voice originated was impossible to say. It seemed to be somewhere above them. Behind the building? On the roof? And it seemed to move around. Or was it coming from the street behind them?

Senator Wainwright grabbed the microphone as though it were his sole support. "No. No. No. I just wanted her to get an abortion."

"Why?" The voice out of nowhere was again deep and sonorous.

"Because she was unfaithful to me."

Oops. That rattled you. I thought that was why you wanted the abortion: so no one would know. Has the good Senator been flummoxed by these voices out of nowhere? Is he blacked out again?

"Unfaithful?" The other place this time. "With who?" Father Wolfe caught himself and held back the reflex act to shout "whom."

"Him. That louse. That wolf in sheep's clothing." The Senator's usual eloquence was wearing thin. He could not draw on the vast lexicon of opprobrium that was politically improper. "Him." And he pointed to the edge of the crowd below him. Father Wolfe looked over. And there on the other side of Captain Parsons stood Jerry Harris. "Him. Jerry Harris.

"He spent the night with my Gina when she was on a trip of goodwill to Los Angeles three weeks ago. I know this from my good friend Doctor Bier here who was there and saw them together at the same convention Gina had attended and saw them go off together. Just to be sure, he phoned her hotel to see if she had checked in that night. She had not. He wanted me to know. For he had suspected this sort of thing for a long time. Good friend."

Suddenly demure Marie Goodwin—her white patch of hair was shiny from the rain—grabbed the bullhorn from Jessica Sommers. "You fool!" She was no longer demure. "I was with her the whole time she was in LA. From the moment she got off the plane at LAX until we returned to Phoenix together. The only time she saw Jerry Harris was at the meeting itself. And that was for five minutes. And I was there with them. The only reason she was not checked in at her hotel was that she was staying with me at my mother's that night. And before God in any court of law I will swear to God that absolutely nothing was going on between them. You fool. You fool." And her obvious anger switched to deep-down sobs. "My Gina. Oh, my little Gina."

SIXTY-FIVE

The deep-down barrel-toned voice again. Where was it? Who was it? "Doctor Aldo Bier..."

"...why did you kill Regina Wainwright?"

"Gotcha there." Doctor Bier turned to the Senator. Did he really think this was God accusing him? "I was with you, Gene. You are my alibi. I was with you the whole time. After you brought Gina in until I returned to find her gone."

"I didn't accuse you." Was the Senator's conscience working overtime? Were all of their consciences straining at the surprising accusations? Did they really think they were listening to an angry God?

The drizzle had turned to an earnest but light rain. Everyone was getting soaked, but no one left. They stood glued to the pavement. Would hell disperse them? Or high water?

Mohandas Patchavar was at Father Wolfe's right side. "Father. Columbo coat. Light hair." He was pointing at Allie Carpenter who was standing on the second floor in front of the office window and right next to the Senator, apparently moving in as soon as possible on the Senator's prestige. "White hair."

And then he started to shout. "Coat. Coat. Hair." And he kept pointing at Allie Carpenter. "Columbo. Columbo."

Allie turned and glared at him. But before she could say anything, the booming voice was back.

"Allie Carpenter, why did..."

"...you kill Regina Wainwright?"

"Me?" Outraged innocence.

"Why would I want to kill her?" The same hard male voice she had used at the soiree.

"Because you yourself at the Senator's soiree insisted that you would do anything—even kill—to have him all to yourself as the Governor's wife." *Did I shout that? And Gerry is here to witness it!*

"You're the one who stole the coumadin." Again the booming voice from beyond.

"What coumadin?"

And back came the tear-soaked rage of Marie Goodwin. "The coumadin I brought back from LA after my mother's death. The coumadin I intended to use myself. Rather than go out and buy more to fill my doctor's prescription."

The deep demanding voice was back. "And how was it the vials with the name Henrietta..."

"...Goodwin were in your bedroom bureau drawer..."

"...empty? All six of them." The voice continued to bounce down from somewhere above the building. And suddenly Father Luke recognized the voices. Of course. Terry and Barry. And they must have bullhorns on different sides of the roof or behind the building. Or maybe they had planned to have that aluminum wrap bounce their voices back and forth. He looked up and smiled. There in the branches of the cottonwoods in the brief parkway that lined Seventh Street and cornered on Mountain that separated the street from the sidewalk were six-foot-square sheets of what looked like Reynolds Aluminum Wrap softly undulating in what little breeze there was. And at least ten of them. How had they managed to get such big sheets? Gluing smaller ones together? Like their experiments in their shop. How had they managed to hang them in the branches of the cottonwoods? They had probably been watching old W. C. Fields movies. And they had succeeded very well in imitating that gravelly voice. If only a touch of its sardonic overtones. Or undertones. It sounded like Moses' God and His thunder.

Suddenly Captain Parsons and Lieutenant Higgins were beside her on the landing. "Allie Carpenter, I arrest you on suspicion of having murdered Regina Wainwright."

As he started to recite her Miranda rights, she turned on him with the face of an angry pit-bull, aflame. Not to be trifled with.

"Arrest me? For murdering Gina? Don't be silly. Why?"

"We'll explain that when we are down at the station. But I assure you that there's enough to send you to prison for long enough to wish you hadn't. Or the hot seat."

Her face went ashen. And her eyes glittered with something you would expect of an angry leopard that has trapped his wildebeest—their brightness was visible even to Father Wolfe fifty feet away. "Well, if I can't have him, no one can."

Before Lieutenant Higgins could draw his Glock from its holster and aim it at her—the captain was in the way—she had pulled a target practice Smith and Wesson .22 out of her "Columbo" coat and fired it twice into Senator Wainwright's chest. He collapsed—as he had three days earlier—like an empty onion sack.

And as she turned to fire at Captain Parsons, she was hit full in the face—just above her right eye—with an extremely hard baseball. A baseball that carried the signatures of Randy Johnson and Curt Schilling.

Joey Fetter had done it again.

And from more like eighty feet this time.

When the paramedics arrived a few minutes later, Senator Eugene Wainwright was very dead.

But only after Father Wolfe had rushed up to the porch and swept a Sign of the Cross over the Senator and uttered the words of conditional absolution. *Lord, bring this mixed-up man to the joy of Yourself. Now.* He wondered if he should start carrying the oil of the sick.

SIXTY-SIX

"Well, we meet again, Father. And again in somewhat unpleasant circumstances. Again. One of these days we'll have to just visit at a nice restaurant. Tommy's? Out on Tocsin and 19th Avenue."

"Yes, Your Honor. I wish these unpleasant circumstances didn't have to occur." He tried to look reproachfully at Terry and Barry. But he couldn't—not under the circumstances.

"Cigar? No, you don't smoke, do you, Father? A little ironic that a Mormon like myself does and shouldn't and you don't and very well could. But then little rules are meant to be broken now and then, aren't they, Father?"

How do you answer an end-around question like that?

"But then I said that the last time we met, didn't I?" Judge Patterson chuckled deep down and unwrapped a Corona he had rescued from the cherrywood humidor on his desk. "A dram of Courvoisier, perhaps?" The Judge chuckled quietly to himself.

Father Wolfe said "No" with an open gesture of his right hand. Like the judge in *High Noon* when he told Gary Cooper to get out while the getting was good. They were in the judge's quarters to the left and behind his courtroom in City Hall. And it was the middle of the afternoon the same day as the Family Freedom protest.

"What are we to do with these two boys, Father?" Even though it was Saturday—the day the judge usually kept as far away as possible from his judicial quarters—at the urging of Captain Parsons the judge asked the relevant parties to appear in order to get this whole business under control.

"Shouldn't their parents...?"

"I have already talked to Mr. and Mrs. Mohr. And they are shocked out of their gourds." Did the judge talk this way from the bench? "In their dismay, I suggested that even though the two of them would live at home, in a special way they should be remanded to your care." He waved the cigar and its gracious puff of smoke toward Father Luke.

"But, Judge, I already have the job of being a super-guardian angel to Larry Curtland. Don't you remember? It was just a month—two weeks—ago I was here with him. And because he had seen the light—he no longer wanted to kill every abortionist he could find—you let him out of jail under my direction."

"Yes, I remember very well, Father. I would have assigned you to be an assistant to the Angel Moroni." He laughed gently from the depths of his more than ample stomach. "But you don't believe in him, do you? Or that he appeared to Joseph Smith?" The droopy jowls bounced a little in silent laughter. "Yes, I know, Father. But after all those years of teaching, I am sure you have your classes well enough prepared to have a little free time you could devote to the moral growth of these two—umm—wayward young men."

Lord, why is it that somehow non-teachers thought all teachers had all sorts of empty hours?

"As I say, I have already talked to their parents. And I have already talked to these two young men."

"And we have promised the judge..."

"...we will do everything you tell us."

"He said he wanted us to swear to that, Father."

"But he said it was OK if we didn't..."

"... and just promised to obey you..."

"...when we told him you had said that..."

"...Jesus taught us never to swear."

Judge Patterson smiled a Christmas Eve-happy-Santa Claus smile.

"How can I say 'No'?" Father Wolfe fumbled with his hair.

"Don't."

SIXTY-SEVEN

Almost time for community Mass. Father Wolfe climbed the front stairs of the Jesuit residence. He had parked the Neon under the ramada behind the residence and had found that somehow his arthritis had left him for the time being as he took long strides to the front entrance.

"Good evening, Father." Mrs. Smedana was at the switchboard and was smiling her genuine toothy smile. She always made it very clear that she loved all the Fathers.

"I was there this morning, Father. Wasn't it just wonderful what your boys did? The twins. And that boy with the ability to throw a baseball like a"— she paused to look for the right word—"cannon. Right between the eyes." Mrs. Smedana glowed a little.

Yes, on Monday they would have to give Joey Fetter another diploma, this time with a big III after the William Tell Award, the way they do for a series of movie titles.

"And who would have thought"—she was just inside the footlights of gushing—"the twins would have been so clever as to play an Old Testament God with those bullhorns? Where did they get them?"

"Mrs. Smedana, I had a thought on the way home this evening. And it concerns you."

Mrs. Smedana made the necessary effort to appear contrite. And to turn her mind from the matter at hand. Her jowls drooped a little.

"No, it's not something bad you have done. It's an opportunity."

She turned her smile back on.

"A young man by the name of Jerry Harris, a very nice young man, needs a nanny, an au pair—no, that's not right. He needs a loving, warm, grandmother to take proper care of his three small children. His wife left him and she hasn't bothered with any kind of visiting rights. And Jerry—he is a very successful lawyer in town—is too busy to take care of them during the day and doesn't want them at a faceless day-care."

Was Mrs. Smedana going to cry? "The poor children."

"I immediately thought of you. And then of Mrs. Goodwin. But you had the daytime job at Family Freedom. And Mrs. Goodwin was beginning to feel the strain of trying to cover for her Gina in all of the programs for others she had become the heart and soul for.

"Good ladies. Both." Father Wolfe stroked the straggling bits of hair on his head. "And now that they must surely be closing Family Freedom, considering how hard it was for them to get Doctor Bier after the murder there two weeks ago and that he will be undoubtedly—umm—de-frocked by the Arizona Medical Board for his admission of complicity in an attempted murder. And this would give you a good-paying job, doing something I suspect you would like. Besides, even if the abortion place does stay open, wouldn't this be a better job for you?"

"Oh, Father, I'd love it. What's Jerry's phone number?"

SIXTY-EIGHT

Chollie,

At supper the guys here thought the whole thing was pretty funny—would I never keep my name and face out of the news?—when I told them what had happened. Was all this just a series of screen tests for a new career in Hollywood? Even though it was another murder. And another abortionist's "good works" hitting the fan for unorthodox medical behavior.

Father Al Friedl plans to use the example of Joey Fetter's fireball and its effects. In his physics classes. What he should demonstrate with it save that two bodies cannot occupy the same space at the same time, I'm not sure. But my un-physics mind is probably missing something here. And I will have to ask Al about this.

When they wanted to know how Parsons knew Allie was the murderer, I told him about that stray bit of information that Parsons had let me in on way back there: in the Gina Wainwright autopsy they had found a slight scratch on her arm that was the source of all the blood. Much too much blood for such a simple scratch. And that's how the coumadin that the Mohr boys found was missing came in. Two days before the scheduled abortion, Allie Carpenter had been lacing everything Gina drank with it—so much so that she would hemorrhage with the slightest encouragement. It was clear she hoped that Doctor Bier would somewhere along the line cut Gina sufficiently to bring about a huge hemorrhaging that not even he could control. And when he had not—that's why Mohandas found it strange that the "black car" driven by the white hair and the Columbo coat had sat quietly across the street before she came up to do the job herself: she wanted to be sure the doctor had done the job. She had seen the doctor leave. And all the lights had gone out—the Patchavars were in a room on the other side of the building. And when nothing was going on, she scratched her just enough to get the blood flowing. She has not confessed to this yet, but Captain Parsons' men are going over the house with every care to see if there is evidence of this that will stand up in court. And already they have discovered coumadin in what was left of a pitcher of iced tea. And in the remains of an unwashed soup bowl. And in an unwashed milk glass. For starters. Allie may have been a good shot and a clever strategist in removing her enemy, but she was anything but a tidy housekeeper.

I wondered if this was all too complicated for table talk. But I looked around and found them all listening intently. In fact, Father Pierre had left his soup at the other table to lean over Al and listen.

So I continued with the whole grisly tale. What had helped matters along, the good Captain told me, was a phone tip the day after the murder. Anonymous—the caller hung up as soon as Mrs. Smedana had understood it and promised to relay it to the Captain. Parsons said "the switchboard lady" insisted it sounded like W. C. Fields. The Mohr boys? They still haven't told me about this part of their escapade.

It told him about the missing coumadin so that he could get a search warrant. But he was able to get it only on the day after the murder.

And of course Mohandas' seeing Gene going into the theater after Doctor Bier had come out to change out of his operating clothes only muddied the waters. Had he planned to stifle her? Was he afraid that Bier would not go through with it—the abortion and the murder? And he had made sure while he could? But his testimony about the "person in the Columbo coat" coming on the scene after the other two had left pretty much nailed it down. When I looked around, I saw that they had all stopped eating. No comments from anyone. All of the guys from the other table were listening, too. Now, how could I transfer this attention to the kids in the classroom?

Well, yes, except for Mrs. Goodwin. That was the postscript. Did Allie know about the inheritance? Or if she did, was she aware of its implications? After all, she had no way of knowing from what Mohandas Patchavar had seen that it could have been either of them.

Gerry Sloan had little to say. But he looked up and eyed the whole table—one after the other. "I was glad I was there to witness all this so that I could see it really had nothing to do with us or Kino. As such." He went back to impaling a slice of tomato in his salad with the tines of his fork.

After reflecting on Bill Blazer's comments about him, I respect him. And all you have to do is watch him for just a little while to know that he is a good priest. And kind, to judge from his understanding reaction to Scott's pain. But I wish he could be a little more gracious.

And I suppose Gerry wishes I could be a little more obedient. And understanding. And humble.

Well, I hope the next week will be quieter than this last month. Four murders is certainly enough for a while. Two—mother and son—from hemorrhaging and freezing. One from a bullet to the heart. And then, Larry Curtland's father by an embolism produced by a syringe injection of air by his partner.

And tell the Lord Jesus to take Gina and Gene right straight to Himself.

Yes, Gene was gone even before the paramedics got there.

And yes, I gave him conditional absolution. As I had his wonderful wife—almost a week earlier.

May he enjoy the presence of his lovely Gina and God Himself now face to face.

Luke

SIXTY-NINE

"Good to see you here again, Father." Mrs. Goodwin was at her warmest.

Father Wolfe was standing outside in front of St. Ignatius Church—shaking hands, chatting, blessing those who had been present at his Sunday Mass—still clad in his alb and chasuble.

"Hello, Mrs. Goodwin."

"It should be *Marie* by this time, shouldn't it, Father?"

"I guess it should be *Luke*, then."

"Oh, Father, I couldn't do that." She smiled and looked at her feet. Like an eight-year-old who had been told that she had just played the piano like a professional.

"I just stopped by to say how—in spite of our loss of wonderful Gina." She stopped. Was she going to cry? She looked up into Father Wolfe's face as if she could find some kind of strength there. "In spite of our loss of Gina, I feel so much more able to accept it now that it's all over and I had my chance yesterday to help to bring justice."

"You certainly were forthright and fearless." And he remembered Father Pierre's story about boyhood courage. "What's going to happen now?"

"Well, Benjy is without parents. At all. At all." She looked off to the elementary school building. "But I'm sure the law will let him be my new son. There certainly is no need to worry about money. Gina—her uncle had been the marvelously successful CEO of Henry Boats—I've told you all this already, Father.

And in her will she left a good hunk of her inheritance to the Senator. And a good part to me. That's why I was a good suspect in the murder—why 'God' didn't insist that I prove my innocence, I do not know. Maybe they felt it would get no reaction from me. And Benjy was in his father's will. Half. The other half would go to Gina. So now he gets it all. But I think I told you all this already.

"We're money OK. But it will take a while to adjust to this terrible loss. Of everything else except money." She paused and looked at the tops of the palm trees a block to the east. "Father, did you know that I was a suspect and would have gone through the terrible experience of jail and all if Allie had not so dramatically focused attention on herself? I ran into Captain Parsons on the way to Mass and he told me."

"Well, yes. There was the coumadin and the will and the Columbo coat and the white hair, Marie. But we all knew that somehow all this did not add up."

"Thank God, Father!"

Yes, thank you, God!

Father Wolfe smiled and patted her on the shoulder.

There was a buoyant lift to her step as she headed for the parking lot.

SEVENTY

"Hiya, Father Wolfe." It was 7:30 on Monday morning, the second day after the big Family Freedom confrontation. It was Tony, of course with his arm around Rita—just before they headed for Mother Teresa. Saturday morning Terry and Barry with Joey Fetter's help had upstaged the police—they had already guessed the identity of the murderer—and had used the phony accusations as a draw—and everyone else's part in the whole sordid business. And Senator Eugene Wainwright was very dead. And the murderer—murderess?—and Doctor Aldo Bier were both behind bars downtown—the latter now officially as an accessory before the fact. "Did you see the show?" It was Tony, of course, there with his arm around Rita at the door of his classroom and on her escorted way to Mother Teresa. "They had the whole Family Freedom business on the late news both Saturday and Sunday."

"Never quite made it to the late news. I've had enough of all that."

"I guess we all have, Father."

With difficulty Father Wolfe unlocked the classroom door—his left arm wrapped around his bulging brief case—testimony that on Sunday after he came back from St. Ignatius Church he had managed to correct all the *Othello* papers and half of the sophomore "Wild Story" essays. When Tony tried to help him, Father shooed him away, saying they had better leave the precarious balance alone. He walked across the room and put his briefcase on his desk.

"Well, it looks as though we won't be demonstrating in front of Family Freedom anymore. Or at least for a while." It was Rita, smiling her quiet but bright happy smile at what God had managed to work out of their protest efforts. "I guess it was envy that did Allie Carpenter and Doctor Bier in. And jealousy that took its toll on the Senator." It sounded as though she had been listening to Tony trying to get the words straight for class.

"Terrific, Rita. That's what I have been trying to get Tony and the rest of his class to understand. Excellent." And he smiled at Tony.

Tony grimaced. Rita gave him a knowing smile.

"Father, we want to thank you...." Tony obviously was trying to distract them.

"Me? You'd better thank Barry and Terry and Joey."

SEVENTY-ONE

Tony looked up at the wall clock. Still time enough to hang out a little longer before he took his Rita to Mother Teresa.

It would be first period according to the schedule. And Joey Fetter and his buddy Dana Poynt were coming in early.

"Why so dejected? Heroes aren't supposed to be sad." Tony was trying to be his avuncular best.

Joey stopped and looked at him. Were those tears in his eyes? There certainly was anger for such a question. "I didn't even make the first cut."

"What cut?"

"The JV baseball cut."

"You're kidding." Father Wolfe was incredulous. "After that spectacular display the day before yesterday, what more did the coach need?"

"He said I wasn't a team player. A prima donna, he said. Who could do spectacular things. But a loner."

"I think we oughta go looking for Mr. Henry." Tony hunched his big shoulders. "Each of us with a bat in his hand. A large baseball bat. And fire in our eyes."

"Oh, come on, Ton." Father Wolfe had turned his stern 'we're all gonna be quiet now, guys' look on him. "Let's just go and tell the coach he should have watched the news the night before last. And suggest he at least go back to the Sunday papers to find out what happened and see that Joey is the best of 'team players.' And point out to him that this is the third time Joey has worried about others."

"Really deep team spirit." Tony smiled a little. "And if he cannot understand that, let's go to Father Sloan and suggest that our baseball coach doesn't have any team spirit. And needs a replacement." And he laughed.

"No, let's just go to our kind-hearted principal. He will, I'm sure, work out a pleasant ending to all this."

And Rita smiled. Her sparkling-eyes smile.

SEVENTY-TWO

"Thank you, Father..."

The two Mohr boys were suddenly standing beside Father Wolfe's desk.

"...for going to bat"—had they been listening?—"for us..."

"...with our parents..."

"...and with Judge Patterson..."

"...and the Dean."

"Did it do any good?"

"Well, you know what the judge said..."

"...and our parents said we wouldn't be grounded..."

"...if we would just do what you said."

Tony smiled—perhaps beamed is a better word—as he looked down at the two of them. "And what did the Dean say?"

"Well, he said that his first thought was..."

"...to let us off completely. Considering."

"But then it wouldn't be fair to others..."

"...since we had skipped four-and-a-half school days. So..."

"...he said we'd have to go to detention after school today..."

"...and write a special essay on how he, the Dean, should go about..."

"...apprehending malingerers."

Tony guffawed. Satisfaction from deep down in his chest.

Rita smiled. Happily.

But Terry wasn't finished. "What's a malingerer, Father?"

Tony laughed again.

"Well." Why did he have to keep repeating himself? "There's always the handy pocket-sized dictionary over there on the shelf."

"You mean the underbridged"—that was his word—"Webster? Pocket-sized if the pocket belongs to Goliath or Paul Bunyan. Or Noah—the guy with the boat full of animals, that is."

Why bother to correct them? Their dictionary will serve them even if it is not really very wet.

"See you in fifth, Father."

Rita waved a little-girl, shell-closing wave. And smiled her radiant smile.

Printed in the United States
40485LVS00001B/257